Ryan nodded, apprec... amazing. You know th..., ...ght?

Addy laughed nervously. "Thanks. Erm...so are you."

For a moment they just continued to stare at one another. The air in the gap between them was taut as a bow, as neither of them knew what to say or do next.

Would he step forward and drop a kiss onto her cheek?

Would he step away and simply say goodbye and give her a cheery wave?

Which one would she prefer? The heat and excitement and danger of the kiss? Or the disappointment of him simply walking away from her? If he kissed her, what would it mean? A simple friendly thank-you? Or something more?

She wanted the excitement and danger of a kiss on the cheek. She wanted the wonder. She wanted the thrill.

Another moment of tension and then suddenly, he stepped forward, placed his hands on her upper arms and leaned in to drop a kiss onto her cheek.

Dear Reader,

The character of Addalyn (Addy) had been taking up space in my brain for years, but I didn't know too much about her, which story to fit her into or which hero would step up to take a place at her side. I was never ready to write her, and each time I had to come up with a new synopsis, I'd pull her character out, brush her off and take another look. Was I ready to write her?

Very often, the answer was no, LOL!

But this time, I began to see a little girl called Carys, who was being raised by a firefighter father—Ryan. And I saw these two, holding hands at the zoo, and from nowhere, Addy stepped in and scooped Carys up into her arms!

Addy was ready. All she'd needed was a little girl to love and a hunky fireman to keep her safe, even though she knew that Ryan represented a danger to her heart.

So, I hope you enjoy Addy and Ryan's story. It's been a long time coming, but for me, the wait was worth it!

Happy reading,

Louisa xxx

FINDING FOREVER WITH THE FIREFIGHTER

LOUISA HEATON

MEDICAL ROMANCE

Harlequin®
MEDICAL
ROMANCE

Recycling programs for this product may not exist in your area.

ISBN-13: 978-1-335-59550-8

Finding Forever with the Firefighter

Harlequin Enterprises ULC
22 Adelaide St. West, 41st Floor
Toronto, Ontario M5H 4E3, Canada
www.Harlequin.com

Printed in U.S.A.

Louisa Heaton lives on Hayling Island, Hampshire, with her husband, four children and a small zoo. She has worked in various roles in the health industry—most recently four years as a community first responder, answering emergency calls. When not writing, Louisa enjoys other creative pursuits, including reading, quilting and patchwork—usually instead of the things she *ought* to be doing!

Books by Louisa Heaton

Harlequin Medical Romance

Yorkshire Village Vets

Bound by Their Pregnancy Surprise

Greenbeck Village GPs

The Brooding Doc and the Single Mom
Second Chance for the Village Nurse

Night Shift in Barcelona

Their Marriage Worth Fighting For

A GP Worth Staying For
Their Marriage Meant To Be
A Date with Her Best Friend
Miracle Twins for the Midwife
Snowed In with the Children's Doctor
Single Mom's Alaskan Adventure

Visit the Author Profile page
at Harlequin.com for more titles.

For Nick

CHAPTER ONE

THIS WAS THE perfect place. To rest. To recharge after a difficult and complicated shout. Here, halfway up Abraham's Hill, there was a clearing amongst the trees and she could look down upon the people in the park. Families sharing picnics. Children playing, giggling, chasing one another. Young couples sitting on the grass. Older ones holding hands, or feeding the birds gathered around their feet. The perfect place to stop thinking about the awful situations people often found themselves in and instead bask in the peace and serenity of happy, content, *safe* ones.

Hazardous Area Response Team paramedic Addalyn Snow yearned for the serenity of happy, content people, but often felt it was a condition that would always somehow be out of her reach. She wasn't bitter about it. It was something she had become resigned to. Her life was filled with drama, both at work and unfortunately, these last few years, at home.

Biting into her chicken salad wrap, she found her gaze captured by a young boy and a girl chasing each other around, laughing, and she didn't notice a dollop of garlic mayonnaise escape from her wrap until it landed on her uniform. She swore quietly and used her finger to wipe it up, licked it, then reached for the wipes that she kept in the glove compartment of her work vehicle. She was just rubbing at her uniform, hoping and praying that the mayo wouldn't stain, when she received a call.

'Three one four, this is Control. We have a report of a situation occurring at Finnegan's Hole in Bakewell. Possible tunnel collapse with multiple casualties. Cave rescue and fire brigade en route. Can you attend, over?'

'Control, this is three one four. Show as attending. ETA…' she glanced at her watch '…fifteen minutes, over.'

'Thank you, three one four.'

Addalyn looked about for a bin to throw the last part of her sandwich into, but the one near her car was already overflowing. So she just stuffed the rest of her sandwich into her mouth, closed the car door and started up the engine, activating the blue lights. She would use the siren when she reached built-up areas and traffic.

She felt some trepidation in her stomach. Finnegan's Hole was a popular potholing site with a narrow entrance. She'd attended a job there once before, as a new paramedic, when a potholer had gashed his leg open on a sharp rock formation. She could remember standing there, looking down at the cave entrance, and wondering why on earth anyone would be crazy enough to do potholing as a hobby. She'd never been fond of enclosed spaces herself, but hadn't realised the extent of this until she did her three-day-long confined space training in her quest to become a HART paramedic.

HART paramedics received extra training. They specialised in providing first responder care in areas considered more hazardous than those a conventional paramedic would operate in, often working alongside multiple other agencies.

Addalyn had worked hard to become a HART paramedic and she loved her job. It meant she had to think carefully about each and every decision. Each and every shout was completely different and no two work days were the same. She often worked long hours, but the best thing about that was that when she got home, exhausted and tired, it meant she could fall into bed and go right to sleep. When she woke up the cycle would begin again, so she didn't have to think too hard about the spaces in between when she was finished for the day and when she had to clock on again. It meant she didn't have to notice how alone she was. Or who she was missing. Or why.

And if those thoughts did creep in she silenced them with food, or the TV, or loud music pumping through her ears as she exercised to retain her fitness levels.

She knew how to push herself hard. It was what

she had always done. Even as a child. And pushing hard, being determined not to let life beat her to a pulp, as it had tried in the last few years, was what kept her going.

Addalyn activated the sirens as she came upon traffic. There was always a lot of traffic in Derbyshire, even in rural areas such as Bakewell or Matlock. Her work covered the area of Derbyshire that contained the Peak District, and it was popular with tourists and walkers. And in this next job's case potholers. The Peak District had a lot of natural pothole formations. Nettle Pot, which was over a hundred and fifty metres deep, Poole's Cavern, a two-million-year-old limestone cavern, and the mighty Titan Cave, near Castleton, which was Britain's biggest cave.

She had to remain alert. Not all pedestrians saw the lights or heard the sirens. Nor all drivers. She had to be constantly alert for all the hazards that might come her way. It had become a learned skill. In life, as well as at work.

'Stay there…' she murmured to herself as a car appeared at a T-junction on her left, praying that the driver would see her and ease back to let her go past first. Thankfully, the driver saw her, and she raised a hand in thanks as she zoomed past.

Finnegan's Hole, her satnav instructed her, was halfway up a mountain on the other side of Bakewell. It was situated on the east face of Mitcham's Steps, another popular tourist attraction, because the hill there was like a stepped pyramid, with a viewing platform on the top. Finnegan's Hole had only been discovered in 1999, and from what she remembered reading, potholers were still mapping out its many caverns, twists and turns, deep into the earth.

A helicopter flew overhead and she became aware of other sirens ahead of her, and on one long stretch of road she saw the disappearing tail-end of a fire engine. It looked as if they might all arrive at the same time.

She radioed through to Control. 'Any update on the Finnegan's Hole job, Control? Do we know the number or types of casualties, over?'

'We do have an update for you. At least four trapped after a confirmed tunnel collapse. Mostly minor injuries, but one caver is said to be trapped beneath the rubble, over.'

'Any other information on that patient, over?'

'Patient is male and trapped about twenty feet beneath the surface, over.'

Addalyn shivered, imagining what that might look and feel like. Trapped beneath the ground, in the dark, in close quarters, dirt and muck in the air, maybe water… Torchlights flashing this way and that, sound echoing, reverberating around you. In pain. Trapped. Unable to move.

'Thanks, Control.'

Her thoughts immediately jumped back to her confined spaces training. She needed to be aware of the topography of the area they'd be working in, maybe find an expert on the tunnels if one was available. She'd have to think about the risk of further tunnel collapse, maybe gaseous emissions could be a danger, or an increase in water levels? Free-flowing solids? And all of this before she could even think about her patient. She knew nothing about him. He might have other medical conditions that she knew nothing about. A condition that would complicate her ability to attend him. And if he were trapped that far down, the big question was…would she have to go down there?

Her vehicle began to ascend the hill road on Mitcham's Steps, its engine roaring, easily taking her up the steep incline, smoothly and expertly. Some hikers were making their way down and moved to the side of the road to hug the verge as she passed.

She saw curious eyes and faces. Saw some stop to watch her pass, even one or two debating going back the way they'd come to watch the drama that was causing all these sirens to be heard, all these emergency vehicles to pass by.

Finnegan's Hole. One mile, she read on her satnav.

The sun was out, at least. It wasn't a grey, drizzly day. They'd have daylight and a bit of warmth to assist them.

When she arrived at Finnegan's Hole she parked and opened her boot to slip on her high-vis vest, her hard hat, and grab her equipment. As she closed the boot she became aware of a fire chief in a white hard hat approaching her. She recognised him. It was her father's friend Paolo. And seeing him walk towards her, in his fireman's garb, reminded her so strongly of how her father and brother had used to look that grief smacked her in the gut, as if she'd been swung at with a wrecking ball.

'Addy. Good to see you. Are you okay?'

She gave him a quick nod, not quite trusting herself to speak yet. It had been over a year, but it still felt so raw. Thankfully, Paolo seemed to understand, and he jumped straight to business.

'We've got seven in total, trapped from a tunnel collapse, and we have communications. Six of them are fine. Minor injuries, cuts, grazes, some bruises. But one potholer is trapped beneath the rubble. Attempts were made to lift off whatever rocks they could, but they had to stop because of risk of further collapse, and apparently there is one large boulder trapping his left leg. They say it doesn't look good. Almost crushed. Cave rescue is here, setting up, and we've got equipment going in right now to secure the cave roof.'

'Okay. Conditions down below?'

'Mixed. It's a tight squeeze, as I'm sure you know, but only a bare inflow of water. Trickles— nothing more. No gaseous emissions, so I don't think we need to worry about the risk of anything blowing up or catching fire. But they're panicking.'

'To be expected. Who have you got on your team that's good with small spaces?'

The chief smirked. 'You know they're all good.'

'What about Charlie?' She'd worked with Charlie before on an entrapment case.

'Off sick. But we do have Ryan Baker. He's new, but extremely good with stuff like this. Used to be in the army. Did a lot of tunnel work.'

'Then he's my guy. Get him in a harness and rope—he's coming in with me, once I've done the risk assessment.'

A new guy. That was good. He'd have no associations with her past.

The chief saluted and jogged off to talk to his team.

A tunnel guy. Army guy. Sounded good.

Addalyn went over to the mountain rescue team member who was co-ordinating his team with fire and rescue regarding the cave supports that were going in.

'How's it looking?'

'Nearly all the supports are in. Just setting up the lighting for you.'

'What can you tell me about this place?'

'It's pretty much what you'd expect. Lots of close quarters. Limestone, mostly. Some bigger caverns as you descend further. Atmosphere is moist.'

'Hazards?'

'There are some sharp rock formations. Stalagmites. Stalactites.'

'Biologics?'

'Nothing to concern you.'

'You're full of pleasant information.'

He smiled. 'I aim to please.'

'I'm going to lead the rescue. One of the fire crew is going in with me.'

'All right. We'll keep in touch with radio. You'll need one of these.' He passed her a hand radio that she slotted into her vest as he clipped her to a guide rope. 'Where's your other guy?'

'Here.'

She turned to give him a smile. A nod. To introduce herself by name, especially since they'd be in close quarters with one another. She liked firefighters. Had an affinity for them. Her father and brother had both been firefighters. She'd even thought that she would be one, too.

But Ryan Baker was not the sort of guy you just had a single glance at. He was not the type of guy you said hello to and then got on with what you were doing.

He was…different. Intense. Handsome.

Three danger zones that instantly made her heart thud painfully in her chest in an alert as his rich chocolate eyes bored into hers.

'Ryan? I'm Addalyn.'

She held out her hand for him to shake, aware

of a tremor in her voice just as she felt a powerful feeling pass through her when he shook her hand and then let go, his dark eyes barely meeting hers.

'Nice to meet you.' He attached himself to the guide rope with strong, square hands.

An army guy. A tunnel guy.

A *firefighter* guy.

No. She wouldn't think about that.

The mountain rescue man gave her the thumbs-up. 'Lights are in. I've got two of my team who will meet you at cavern two. The tunnel collapse is just ahead of them.'

'All right.'

'Just follow the guide rope down. There will be cameras for you to use when you near the tunnel breach. Go in feet first. There's a small cavern about ten feet down, where you can move around and begin to crawl deeper in.'

'Perfect. Thank you.'

She eyed the small hole in the earth, that basically looked like it was the entrance to a badger sett or something. It didn't look like anything humans should be climbing down into, but she and Ryan would have to go. It was dark. Shadowy. It gave her the shivers, but she knew she could deal with it.

She took a step forward, then felt a hand on her arm.

'I'll go first,' suggested Ryan.

She looked at him and nodded briefly. Her heart

was pounding so fast because of her claustrophobia, wasn't it? Nothing to do with him.

'I'll show you where to put your hands.'

She nodded. 'Thanks.'

He went in feet first, as instructed. Finnegan's Hole swallowed him up easily and he had no hesitation about heading into the dark. She watched him disappear.

People often joked that they wished the earth would swallow them up, but they wouldn't say it if they truly knew how it felt, she thought, following him down, her eyes taking a moment to adjust to the darkness. There were lanterns, as the mountain rescue guy had said, but they were spaced far apart and there were sections as they climbed down where the only light was provided by their head torches.

Her hands touched rock. Her boots found purchase on ledges and outcrops and her body scraped along the tunnel sides, where it got narrow. She tried to push images of this tunnel caving in on her away, knowing she needed to trust in the facts that she had been told: tunnel supports were in place.

Sounds began to carry towards her through the tunnels and caverns. Voices. Some shouting. Others trying to soothe and calm. The dripping of water. The echoes of everything.

Something skittered across the back of her hand and she yelled.

Ryan looked up at her. 'You okay?'

His concern for her was touching, but she was here to help someone. Not to be another person who would need rescuing. 'Fine.'

He squinted, as if deciding to trust that she was telling the truth.

'Honestly. I'm fine. Just not fond of spiders, that's all.'

'Stay by me.'

She had no plans to do anything else.

They descended into the cavern, with Ryan holding out his hands to help her down onto the cave floor. It was a decent size. About the size of her bathroom at home. Tall enough to stand up in. Ahead of them was a small crawlspace, lit with lamps.

Have I got to go in there?

'It shouldn't be far. Remember the mountain rescue guys are in the next cavern already.'

Addalyn nodded. Her mouth had gone incredibly dry, yet the rest of her was sweating, and her heart was hammering away in her chest. All she could feel was a sense of pressure all around her. The pressure that might be on the rock walls. The floor. The ceiling. And if she crawled into that space...

'Addalyn?'

She looked at Ryan.

'You can go back if you want.'

The temptation was immense. It would be so easy, wouldn't it? To just start climbing back in the other direction. Towards the surface. Towards the sunshine and the light and the fresh air. To space and freedom and peace.

But there was a man in trouble who needed her. A man who needed her medical expertise. She couldn't walk away from him, no matter what.

'No. I'm doing this.'

He nodded, a slight smile playing around his beautiful mouth, and that smile was enough. That smile said, *I believe in you. I'm proud of you.*

She thought of her father. Her brother. She was not going to die like they had. 'Let's do this.'

Ryan grinned. 'All right.'

He got down on his hands and knees and began to crawl into the tunnel. As his feet disappeared into the shadows she sucked in a determined breath and followed after him, trying to ignore all that she felt digging into the soft flesh of her belly, or the way her helmet would knock into the rock above her head. Her clothes were wet and dirty and her kit bag, being dragged behind her, must be in a terrible state.

They crawled for what seemed like an age, towards the lights and noises ahead, and then suddenly, in front of her, Ryan was getting to his feet and turning to help her up. His hand reaching for her. She ignored how it felt to take it. Then they were in the second cavern with two of the mountain rescue team.

'Ryan. Addalyn.' Ryan made the introductions.

'Raj. Max,' said one of the men, doing likewise. 'And this lovely gent down here, in need of your help, is John. John Faraday.'

John lay on his back on the cavern floor, his left leg trapped under an immense rock and some rubble. Around him sat the other cavers, two men and a woman. They all looked scuffed and dirty, muddy and frightened. John was pale, but conscious. He lifted a hand in greeting.

'We didn't want to leave him,' the woman said. 'We come down together. We go up together. That's our motto.'

'Sounds good to me,' said Addalyn. 'Now, let's see how we can do this. Ryan? Would you check these guys over whilst I look at John?'

'Sure.'

She knelt by John, took his hand and squeezed it. 'Hey, how are you doing?'

'I've had better days.'

'I bet. On a scale of one to horrible, do you want to tell me how much it hurts?'

'Surprisingly, not much.'

That was probably the adrenaline, keeping him numb.

'I'm going to get a line in to give you some painkillers anyway, just in case. You allergic to anything, John?'

It helped her to focus on her patient. It stopped her being aware of what was all around her, pressing down.

'Just my ex-wife.'

She smiled. She liked him. It took a lot to remain upbeat in a situation such as this.

'This should help.'

She gave him a shot of painkiller, then hooked up a bag of intravenous fluids.

Ryan knelt beside her. 'Just cuts and bruises on the others. They missed the worst of it because John, here, pushed them out of the way.'

'Hero, huh? We need them to go to the surface.'

He nodded. 'Agreed. What do we know about the three trapped behind the rubble?'

One of the mountain rescue guys spoke. 'They're okay. Just John got badly hurt.'

'Okay.' Addalyn stood, stretched her legs. 'I know these guys want to stay and help John, but we need them to go up. That way we can work better on getting John out and opening up the tunnel for the others too. Besides...' her voice dropped low '... I'm not sure they're going to want to see what comes next.'

Mountain rescue nodded. 'I'll get them out.'

Addy knelt back down to John, her gaze taking in his position, his leg beneath the rock, his foot sticking out on the other side. 'Can you wiggle your toes for me?'

'I'll try.' John concentrated and looked up at her hopefully. 'Did my foot move?'

'No. I'm afraid not.' Grim, she reached past

him, squeezing past the boulder. 'Can you feel me touching you?' She stroked just above his ankle.

'No.'

The boulder was massive. His leg beneath it had to be crushed and there would be no way to save it.

Loosening his boot, she tried to feel for a pedal foot pulse, but nothing would register and the foot was cold. She sat back on her haunches.

'John, what kind of support do you have at home?'

'I live with my girlfriend. She's a nurse. She's gonna be so angry with me about this.'

Addy gave him a sympathetic smile, then turned to Ryan. 'Any chance this boulder could be lifted quickly?'

'We could get equipment in, to either remove it or break it up into smaller manageable pieces, but it would take time.'

'How much time?'

Ryan shrugged. 'As much as I'd like to say it could be done quickly, in these conditions it might take time to manoeuvre it through those crawl spaces before we could get set up. But even if we removed it, wouldn't he be at risk for compartment syndrome?'

She was impressed that he would know about it. Compartment syndrome was a condition that occurred in incidents like these, when pressure within the muscles built to dangerous levels. That pressure could lead to decreased blood flow and prevent nourishment and oxygen reaching the tissues. Which, in turn, could lead to a build-up of toxins, so that when the pressure was removed, those toxins would flood the heart and cause the patient to go into cardiac arrest.

'I could do a fasciotomy, but that would just prolong the agony long term.'

A fasciotomy was an emergency procedure performed to try to prevent compartment syndrome. It involved making an incision along the fascia to relieve tension and pressure in tissue.

'Addalyn? You don't have to whisper. Just tell me straight,' said John.

She knelt beside him once again. 'Your leg isn't great, John. It has a severe crush injury with a lot of soft tissue avulsion and high levels of contamination. Your foot has no pulse, and it is also cold and does not move. Your blood pressure is low and you're the wrong side of fifty.'

Her patient swallowed. 'None of that sounds good.'

'It isn't. I'm sorry, but I'm pretty sure a doctor is going to want to perform an expedient procedure on your lower leg.'

She watched his face carefully, having avoided the word amputation, but knowing it was implied. No medic liked telling a patient bad news. But it was something she'd hardened herself to. She couldn't allow doubts and recriminations any room in her mind these days. She already had enough to deal with. So she steeled herself.

'Will it hurt?'

'No. The doctor would put you under. You won't feel a thing. And me and Ryan are going to help take care of you and get you back up to the surface afterwards.'

John looked at Ryan, then back to Addy. 'Have you seen many of these before?'

'Yes.' He didn't need details. He just needed to know this wasn't her first time. 'Everyone is going to do their best for you, John, okay?'

He nodded. 'Before they put me under…can I ask you to tell my girlfriend something? Just in case.'

'You'll be able to tell her yourself when you wake up in hospital. But sure… Just in case.' She leaned in to hear.

'Tell her that I love her and that she made my life the best that it ever could be.'

She looked him in the eyes. 'I will. But everyone's got you, okay?'

'Okay.'

Just then more of Ryan's fire crew arrived, this time with a doctor in tow. Addalyn apprised Dr Barrow of the situation, he confirmed the necessity for the procedure, and made quick work of removing John from his left leg, bandaging him and stabilising him for removal back up to the surface.

Dr Barrow went first, then Ryan took the front

of John's stretcher, whilst his crew mate Tom took the rear. Addalyn followed them up, keeping an eye on the monitoring equipment and hoping that John didn't choose to have a further medical crisis whilst stuck in a small tunnel. Thankfully, he remained stable all the way, and they all emerged on the surface, dirtied, muddied and relieved, before passing John off to an ambulance that would take him to hospital.

Addalyn turned to see Ryan heading back into Finnegan's Hole. 'Where are you going?'

'There are still people down there.'

'I know, but surely it's someone else's turn to go down?'

'That's not how this works.' He smiled, disappearing into the earth a second time.

Addy called through to Control and apprised them of the situation. 'One patient has been medically evacuated, but there are still three trapped behind the collapse. I've been informed that they don't have any serious injuries, but as this is still a multi-operational job, I'd like to stay on scene and be of some help, over.'

'Thank you, three one four. Received. Stay safe out there.'

'I will. Over and out.'

CHAPTER TWO

IT TOOK THREE hours to dig out the tunnel safely and free the rest of the potholers, who were mightily relieved to see some friendly, helpful faces on the other side of the rubble.

Their cuts and bruises were as to be expected, though one of the potholers, a young woman, had a suspected fractured forearm. Ryan splinted it and then followed the others out through the tunnels and into the fresh air, where the sky was blue and the air was warm and welcome.

'Addy? I've splinted this lady's arm. I think she might have a fracture.'

'I'll take a look.'

He was glad to see Addalyn was still there, waiting for him to come out. There'd been no need for her to stay. After all the main casualty, John, had been evacuated many hours before, and the other patients had only mild injuries that wouldn't even require a visit to hospital. And there were other paramedics here. Other ambulances.

She could have left.

But she hadn't.

And he had to admit it felt quite good to see

someone looking so relieved when he emerged safe and sound.

He barely knew Addy. Had met her only today. But they'd been through something dangerous together and that bonded people in a way that no one else would be able to understand, so he knew he'd look forward to working with her in the future.

Finnegan's Hole would now be closed to the public until the tunnels and caverns could be confirmed as stable and safe.

Ryan checked in with his chief, then headed over towards Addy to thank her before he left. She was helping the lady with the injured arm into an ambulance, standing back as the doors closed.

'Thanks for staying.'

She turned to smile at him. A beautiful smile.

'It was my job.'

'Yes, it was, but even so... I appreciate you still being here now we've got everyone out.'

'"*We come down together, we go up together.*" I think I heard that somewhere,' she said with a smile, repeating the words of one of the potholers. 'Besides, I have this thing about keeping an eye on firefighters.'

'Oh?' He gave an amused raise of one eyebrow.

She smiled at him. 'Long story.'

'Best ones are. Listen, I've just spoken to the chief and we're all heading to the Castle and Crow for an evening of decompressing, fine ales and a trivia quiz. You and your team are all welcome to join us.'

He thought she'd say no. He thought she'd say she'd think about it. Or she'd try to make it. Any of those excuses. But it wasn't as if he was asking her out on a date. This was a group thing. It had been a long day, and this last job had been a tough and exhausting one. All he wanted was to have a shower, some food and then an early night, but he also knew of the restorative power of a night out with his crewmates. Decompressing, destressing, having fun and laughing was crucial to help deal with their long hard days on the job. And tonight was a good night to do it. His daughter, Carys, was with his parents for a sleepover.

To his surprise, she said, 'Sounds great! I'll ask the others.'

'Perfect. I'll see you later, then.'

She gave him a nod and turned to head back to her rapid response vehicle. She was still in the clothes she'd been in when she'd gone below with him. The mud had dried out.

'Hey, listen...' He hadn't known he was going to say anything else until his mouth had opened up and begun to spurt sounds. He thought rapidly as she turned to face him again, a look of query on her face. 'You did great down there today. I know you weren't exactly fond of being in such a confined space.'

She smiled and nodded. 'I wasn't, but...thanks.'

He wasn't sure exactly how to end the conversation now. Nod? Say goodbye again? Give her a little wave?

No, that would be weird. Why does it matter? What's got into you? Just walk away, Ryan.

Why had he suddenly become tongue-tied? The last time he'd been tongue-tied had been ages ago. When, exactly?

He frowned, and when the memory came he felt bad.

He'd been tongue-tied when he'd watched his bride, Angharad, walk down the aisle towards him. She'd looked so beautiful in her stunning white gown, holding that bouquet of summer flowers before her as she'd walked to the sound of the 'Wedding March', and just seeing her had seemed to stop all his normal bodily functions from working. His mouth had gone dry, his brain had emptied of all possible thought and reason, and all he'd been able to get himself to do was continue to breathe and try not to cry.

Addy looked nothing like Angharad. She was muddy, rumpled, her hair sprouting loose tendrils around her tired face, but there was something about her...something that called to him. What was it?

It doesn't matter. She's just a colleague. I probably won't see her again for a while after tonight. I can just enjoy her company and not think too hard about it.

'I'll see you tonight, then?'

Another nod. Another smile. Her eyes were *stunning*.

'You can count on it.'

'Great. I'll…er…' He pointed in the direction of the fire engine. Saw the amusement in her gaze and laughed at himself as he walked away.

Addy pushed open the doors to the Castle and Crow. It was one of Derbyshire's tiniest pubs, situated in what had used to be the gatehouse to a castle that now stood in ruins. She'd been, oh, so glad to get the invitation—anything to keep her out of that empty and now silent house.

She wasn't a fan of that silence. It felt thick and heavy. It made the house seem…lifeless. And somehow, though she was the only one living, she felt like a ghost, haunting its rooms, looking for life to latch on to. She missed her dad. She missed Ricky. The empty spaces where they'd usually sat felt cruelly difficult. Dad by the window in the recliner he'd loved so much. Ricky stretched out on the couch, playing video games.

Gone.

Taken from her so quickly.

They'd been her whole world, her security blanket, her soft place to fall after all that horrible business with Nathan, and just as she'd begun to shine again…just as she'd begun to smile and laugh again…life had snatched them both away.

It hurt to be in the house.

Music greeted her as she pushed through the doors and then smiles and cheers as some of the ambulance and fire crew greeted her, insisting she join them at their table. She made the international gesture that said *I'll just grab a drink... anyone else want one?* by pointing at the bar before making her way back over to them armed with a gin and tonic.

Chrissie and Jools had a seat open next to them, so she sat there. 'Hi, guys.'

Chrissie was a paramedic and Jools was an emergency care assistant. On the table next to them were some of the fire crew guys. Paolo, Brewster, Tom and—her heart thudded quicker—Ryan.

She raised her glass to them all. 'So, what are we doing?'

'Pub quiz,' said Chrissie. 'Ambulance versus Fire versus everyone else, I guess. Thatch is in the loo, but he's going to help make up our four.'

Thatch was one of the 999 call takers who worked at Control.

'Great.' Addy took a sip of her drink. 'I always knew all that trivia Dad used to give me would come in handy one day.'

It had been her dad's thing. Every day at dinner he would present her and Ricky with a fun fact for the day. Even when she'd moved back in with them after her split with Nathan. Sometimes it would be hilarious, sometimes intriguing, but it always sparked conversation, and dinner times Chez Snow had quickly become her favourite time of the day.

Nowadays dinner was a ready meal heated in the microwave and eaten in silence in front of the TV. Addy would do her best and watch a quiz shows if she could, whilst eating, but it never quite took away the fact that she was eating alone and that the two seats that would normally be filled with two strong, hearty men were actually empty.

Paolo nodded. 'Ah, yes, Vic knew a thing or two. Where did he get his facts, Addy? Novelty toilet paper?' He laughed and took a sip of his pint, raising his glass in a mock salute to the dead and the lost.

She smiled. 'I don't know. He picked them up from somewhere.'

'Victor Snow?' Ryan asked.

Addy nodded.

'I've seen his picture in the fire station. Ricky's too. I didn't realise you were related. I'm sorry for your loss.'

'Thank you.'

A strange atmosphere settled around the table, with no one quite sure what to say to change the subject, or even if changing the subject was the right thing to do. They all knew what had happened. They all knew what she'd gone through. With maybe the exception of Ryan.

Thankfully it was broken by the return of Thatch from the toilets.

'I'd give the restroom a miss for five minutes, guys. I think I had a dodgy kebab at midday.'

Everyone burst into laughter and Thatch looked around him, not quite sure that his joke had been that funny, or original, but appreciative all the same.

Behind them, at the bar, one of the barmen switched on a microphone and notified them that the quiz would start in ten minutes and that someone would come round with paper and pens momentarily.

Addy took a moment to catch up with Chrissie and Jools. She'd not seen them since the job at Finnegan's Hole that afternoon, and she asked them if they'd had any other interesting shouts.

'A guy who thought he was about to go into a diabetic coma.'

'You got to him in time?'

'He wasn't even a diabetic, Addy! Not been diagnosed—nothing. His blood sugars were fine, but when we looked up his deets on the tablet we could see the guy is constantly visiting his doctor, day after day after day.'

'Health anxiety?'

She nodded. 'We had to check him over, though. The only thing we found wrong was a slightly elevated heart rate, but that was probably down to his stress.'

'Poor guy. Must be hard to live with a condition like that.'

'I think he's lonely, too. Lives alone. Has done for years. The place had a feeling of neglect, you know?'

Addy could sympathise. When she'd lost Dad and Ricky, she'd found it hard to keep up with maintaining the house. Especially because she'd worked as many hours as she could so that she didn't have to be in that empty house. And the more and more things piled up, the worse she felt. But this last year, on New Year's Eve, she'd made a resolution to get on top of things with the house. She'd put on some music, or listen to a podcast, or an audiobook, she'd told herself, and work for fifteen minutes.

Today I'm going to tidy and sort that corner by Dad's chair.

This time I'm going to go through that wardrobe and get rid of the clutter at the bottom.

It was easier in short, manageable bursts. Not so overwhelming. And there'd even been a moment, when the house had begun to look better, brighter, when she'd been proud of herself. The depression and the grief had lifted enough for her to see good things in life again.

It still didn't make it any easier to be home alone, though. She wasn't sure she'd ever get used to living that way.

'Welcome, everyone, to the Castle and Crow

quiz night! We've got some amazing prizes for our winners and our runners up. For the team that places second there is a lovely prize of six bottles of wine, donated by the Tutbury Vineyard, along with tickets to a wine-tasting evening. But for our winners—drumroll, please...'

The clientele all began a low drumming on their tables, building to a crescendo and stopping only when Natalie, the pub landlady, who had the microphone, raised her hands, laughing.

'For our winning team there is a prize kindly donated by the local zoo. Free tickets for six people alongside a zookeeper experience and a meal, drinks included, at their onsite restaurant, Reservation!'

Addy's friend Chrissie leaned in. 'A zoo? No, thanks. I get itchy just thinking about fur.'

Addy smiled.

'So, get your pens and pencils ready!'

Addalyn grabbed her pen and then happened to look up at the fire crew's table. Her gaze met Ryan's and she smiled at him before looking away. She would have quite happily sat at their table. The fire crew had long been a part of her family because of her dad and Ricky. And Ryan seemed nice. Dangerously nice. But he was a fireman, so that made him off-limits.

'First question! What is considered the most dangerous bird in the world?'

Most dangerous bird...? thought Addy.

Chrissie leaned in and whispered, 'Would that be a bird of prey, do you think?'

Addy didn't think so. It might be the obvious choice, but she felt sure she knew the right answer. She just couldn't think of it.

Jools added, 'An emu? They can hurt you if they kick you.'

And then the answer came like a bolt of lightning. 'It's the cassowary,' Addy whispered.

'The what?' Chrissie frowned.

'Lives in Australia. Claws like daggers. Trust me, it's the cassowary.'

'Okay, but if you're wrong, you owe me a glass of wine.'

Addy knew she wasn't wrong. She remembered her dad telling her. One of his fun facts for the day. They'd been discussing flightless birds, and the only ones she and Ricky had been able to come up with had been penguins and kiwis. The cassowary was apparently bigger and stronger and infinitely more dangerous to humans.

'Question two… Which planet has a pink sky?'

Addy looked blankly at Thatch, Jools and Chrissie.

'Mars is the red planet,' said Thatch. 'Could be that.'

'We don't have any other answer. Let's write it down.'

They continued on through the questions, with the quiz pausing at half-time for people to use the loo and order more drinks. Addy was waiting at the bar when Ryan came alongside her.

'Hey,' he said.

'Hey, yourself. How are your team getting on?'

'Not bad, I think. We may be in with a chance of winning.'

'Confident! I like it.'

He laughed. 'It's either confidence or arrogance. Take your pick.'

'Well, you seem like a nice guy to me, so I'll say confidence to be kind.'

'How's your team doing?'

'Good. Though Chrissie has to leave in ten minutes, because her babysitter is on a school night, and Thatch is too busy chatting up that girl in the green dress over there by the pool table, so I think the second half might be just me and Jools.'

'Ah. The fickleness of friends. Who knew the promise of a day at the zoo wouldn't be enough to hold people in their place?'

She laughed. 'A day at the zoo sounds amazing to me. I love animals.'

'Me too.'

He turned to smile at her. A genuinely warm smile. His eyes were bright with happiness and she felt it again. That punch to the gut…that pull in his direction. It disturbed her, so she distracted herself by trying to get the barman's attention to ask for an extra packet of crisps.

'Well, good luck for the second half.'

She grabbed her and Jools's drinks, gripped the crisp packet corners between her teeth, and walked back to her table, her heart still fluttering from having been in Ryan's presence.

He was easy to be with. Easy to talk to. He made her nervous, yes, but it was a *good* nervous. An exciting nervous. It was something she would have to be in control of, but she knew she couldn't avoid him. They worked in the field of emergency response—they would most likely meet lots of times now that he was with Blue Watch.

'Everybody ready? Okay… Question number sixteen… What object will a male penguin give a female penguin to try and romance her?'

There was some muted chuckling and whispered answers. One team shouted out a rude one, to a chorus of giggles, but Addy simply smiled and wrote down the answer—a pebble.

'How long are elephants pregnant?'

The questions got more and more intense, and when the quiz was done the answer sheets were collected in for marking.

Jools grabbed her coat and stood up. 'Well, I've got to go.'

Addy looked up at her in surprise. 'But we've not got the results yet! You can't leave me here alone.'

'You've got the fabulous men and women of Blue Watch to sit with.'

'They're the enemy!' she said, with a laugh.

'They love you. They're your family. Sit next to Ryan. There's space there. Ryan? You don't mind if Addy sits next to you, do you?'

He looked at her. Smiled. 'Of course not.'

That smile was everything. Drawing her in until her anxiety put up a wall.

'But what if we win?' she asked Jools. 'I think we're in with a good chance.'

'Then you go to the zoo and have your meal at Reservation! Zoos aren't my thing. They always leave me feeling sad. But, hey, if we're runners up I wouldn't mind having one of those bottles of wine.'

And with that Jools slung her bag over her shoulder, dropped a kiss on Addy's cheek and sauntered out through the door.

Flabbergasted, Addy turned and looked at Blue Watch, who made welcoming motions with their arms and invited her to sit with them. Nervously, she took her drink over to their table and settled into the seat next to Ryan.

'Thanks.'

'You're one of us by all accounts, anyway. An honorary fire crew member.'

Addy blushed even though he was right. She did still feel that these guys were her family. Paolo, the chief, had worked with her father for a long time. He had served with him and was now near retirement. He'd also been chief to Ricky. They'd all been close. She thought nothing of calling into the station to say hi, if she was passing by.

Nervously, she glanced at Ryan, and caught him looking at her. 'How long have you been a fireman?' she asked, knowing she needed to say something, and that was the only question that popped into her brain.

'About four years.'

'But you were in the army before—is that right?' she asked, recalling what Paolo had told her at Finnegan's Hole.

'Yes, I was.'

'What made you leave the army, if you don't mind my asking?'

'Not at all. I was married and my wife didn't like it. Said she felt isolated. Like she was a single woman. She didn't want to feel like a single parent when she learned that she was expecting.'

'Oh, you have a child?'

She could almost feel herself relaxing. If he was married with a child, then she didn't have to worry about whether he was attracted to her or not.

He smiled. 'Carys. She's five.' He reached into his back pocket and pulled out his phone and showed her a picture.

The little girl was the spitting image of her father. Same dark hair, same chocolate eyes. A wide smile. 'She's beautiful.'

'I think so, but then I'm biased.'

'Is your wife looking after her this evening?'

His eyes darkened slightly. 'No, she's with her grandparents for a sleepover.'

'Oh. Your wife didn't want to come out tonight?'

He shook his head, a grim smile upon his face. 'I'm no longer married to Angharad.'

Single?

'Oh?' She felt nervous again. 'I'm sorry to hear that.'

'She…er…wasn't cut out for motherhood. She thought it was something she wanted, but when Carys arrived she realised that being a parent was harder than it looked and that it required a significant amount of personal sacrifice that she wasn't willing to make. So she left.'

Addy stared at him in surprise. She couldn't imagine walking away from her own child. Being a mother was all that she'd ever wanted. Something she'd chased with singular determination at one point in her life. But nature had let it be known that she would probably never get her dream. She had been unable to get pregnant when she'd been with Nathan, and tests had not shown why. Unexplained infertility had placed a huge toll on their relationship and Nathan had sought solace in the arms of another. Someone who would give him the child that he wanted, leaving Addy alone and desolate and having to move back in with her father and brother.

'I'm sorry. How old was Carys when her mother…?' She didn't want to say *left*.

'About sixteen months.'

'Oh. That must have been difficult...'

How did any woman walk away from her child? Her own flesh and blood...made with the man that she'd loved? She tried to understand. Tried to imagine what might have made her leave. It could have been anything, and she was in no place to judge.

'It was. But I got through it, and Carys and I are good.'

'Does she ask about her mother?'

'Sometimes. She misses having one—I know that. I try to be everything that she needs, but... it's not the same.'

Addy wanted to offer him some comfort. Maybe place her hand on his in a show of compassion. But she was scared to do so. Her life might have been in his hands this afternoon, but she still felt unable to reach out and let him know that she understood his pain, and that she was sorry he was experiencing it.

'I'm sure she'll be fine.'

They were stopped from talking any more when Natalie switched the microphone back on and it made a high-pitched sound. Everyone winced.

'Whoa! Sorry everyone!' she laughed. 'The results are in!'

Addy took a sip of her drink. All of her team were gone except for Thatch, who was technically still there in the pub, just not with her. He seemed to have been successful in his wooing of the woman in the green dress, as they were now sitting together, drinking and flirting with one another.

'It was a close-run thing, ladies and gentlemen, with just one point separating first and second place!'

The crowd whooped and cheered, and when the noise had settled down Natalie gripped the microphone and said, 'In third place, with twenty-one points, we have Team Eclipse!'

There was another cheer and applause.

'And in second place, with twenty-five points, and winning the six bottles of wine with a wine-tasting experience at the Tutbury Vineyard, we have Team Blue Watch!'

Addy clapped hard and beamed a smile at them all.

'And in first place, with twenty-six points, and winning the family zoo ticket, the zookeeper experience and dinner and drinks at Reservation restaurant, we have Team 999!'

Addy gasped in joy and surprise as everyone began to applaud. Briefly she stood and took a bow, this way, then that, before Natalie came over and presented her with an envelope containing her prize.

'Has to be redeemed by the end of this month, I'm afraid,' Natalie whispered, before smiling and walking away, back to the bar.

'Well done, Addy!' said Paolo.

'Yeah, well done,' said the others in chorus, including Ryan.

'It was a team thing,' she said graciously, wondering what on earth she'd do with a family ticket to the zoo when she didn't have a family. Well, she had Blue Watch… Paolo had four grown-up kids, but the others were single. Except Ryan…

She held out the envelope to him. 'You should have this. You and Carys.'

Ryan looked at her in surprise. 'But you won.'

'I don't have a family to take to the zoo. You do.'

Hesitantly, he reached for the envelope, but as he held it he looked at her. 'On one condition.'

'What's that?'

'You come with us.'

CHAPTER THREE

IT HAD BEEN the right thing to do, hadn't it? Asking Addalyn to go with them to the zoo?

It was a question that kept rattling through his brain the day before they were due to go, as he and Blue Watch raced towards a road traffic incident on the motorway.

The call had come through eight minutes ago. A multi-vehicle pile-up, after a tree had come down in the strong winds they were having.

Would Addy be there? She might be, if she was on duty today. He'd not seen her since the Castle and Crow pub quiz, when she'd very kindly gifted himself and Carys the family ticket to the zoo.

Carys had been so happy when he'd told her about the day out they were going to have at the zoo. His daughter loved animals! She particularly had an affinity for tigers, and had two cuddly toy versions that slept in her bed with her—Tigger and Joey. And if there was a nature documentary on the television she'd much rather watch that than any cartoon or movie. He loved her confidence and thirst for knowledge, and nurtured it at every turn. So to be offered tickets to the zoo, where

Carys could see tigers in real life and pretend to be a zookeeper…? Of course he'd accepted!

It had felt only right to invite the real winner of the prize along. Addy had said she had no family, but from what he understood she was an honorary member of Blue Watch because of her father and brother. So of course he'd insisted she go with them.

But it would only be as friends, even though he did feel attracted to her. How could he not? She was beautiful, inside and out. Dark, almost black, straight hair. Large chocolate-brown eyes, underlined by darker shadows that hinted at bad sleep patterns, and full, soft pink lips in a very pale face. The kind of pale that if you saw it in a movie, you'd imagine her as a vampire. Because even though she had an outdoorsy job, she looked as if she'd never gone out in the sunlight. Yet she was strong and funny and kind. Generous, clearly. Warm-hearted. And clever—he couldn't forget that.

She looked as if she needed a good day out, and he knew Carys was chatty and confident enough with strangers for it to not be awkward.

'We're going to have a lady with us,' he'd told her. *'Her name is Addalyn.'*

'Addalyn? She sounds like a princess.'

'I guess she is, in a way. She looks after people. She's a paramedic, but her daddy and her brother were firefighters like me.'

'Is she pretty?'

'I guess so.'

'Is she your girlfriend?'

He'd smiled at his daughter's questioning, before shaking his head.

'Do you want her to be your girlfriend?'

Carys had chuckled and snuggled into him on the couch, leaving him with a question that had been on his mind lately. When Angharad had left, he'd sworn never to be with a woman ever again. Especially one who wasn't committed. But would he one day be ready for a relationship? With his daughter in tow? He refused to expose Carys to any woman who wouldn't love his daughter as much as she loved him, and he just wasn't sure there were any woman like that out there. Or, more truthfully, any that he could trust. He'd already been burned, and he wouldn't do so again.

'Coming up on the site. Game mode, guys,' said Paolo from the driving seat of the fire engine.

Ryan looked through the windscreen to the accident site up ahead. Police were already there, blocking off traffic and sending it down the outside lane only, to help ease some of the tailback. Lights flashed, and on the side of the motorway he could see one or two people from various vehicles, clearly unhurt. Behind them he heard more sirens as ambulances approached, but he had no time to look as he fastened his helmet and clambered from the vehicle to receive instructions from Paolo.

He was to go and help secure a white transit van that was on its roof, teetering in the gale-force winds that were still blowing. Steam was issuing from its underside, where a radiator must have been broken, and the driver was still trapped inside. The vehicle needed securing so that the patient could be safely extracted without causing further harm to himself or to the other rescuers that were turning up on-scene.

He collected the wedges that would provide primary stabilisation for the vehicle, whilst his colleague Matt began to attach the struts. The winds were strong, and they didn't need the vehicle moving whilst they attempted an extraction.

And then he heard her voice.

Addalyn.

He turned to look, saw her with Paolo, organising the scene. She was saying who should go where, and triaging the remaining drivers and passengers with injuries as she strode towards the vehicle he was working on. She knelt down by the driver, who was unconscious and had a lot of blood dripping from his head onto the roof of his car. He was held in place by his seatbelt. She checked his pulse and called for a head collar from the paramedic who had rushed to her side to assist. Ryan watched her carefully attach the collar, talking all the time to her patient, explaining everything she was doing even though the man was unconscious.

He respected her for that. The trapped, injured man wasn't just a piece of meat, but a person, and whether he could hear her or not she clearly wanted him to know what was happening to him, just in case. Who knew what the unconscious mind retained? This man, if he survived, might have dreams years into the future of a woman's voice reassuring him in disturbing times and might later wonder what his dreams meant.

'Ryan? We need you to cover the spill from that motorhome and secure the gas canisters inside.'

He saluted Paolo and ran to attend to his next job. The motorhome was on its side, all passengers and the driver having escaped the vehicle. But these motorhomes had kitchens, with little gas stoves in them, and they needed to be fed from pressurised gas canisters.

Some motorhomes carried only one, others two.

And they were an explosive hazard that needed to be removed.

Addy looked up from her patient and watched as Ryan ran to contain the gas. A part of her wanted to reach out, grab his arm and haul him back. Say, *No, not you. You have a daughter. Let someone else go. I need you.*

She was shocking herself with her thoughts.

Someone had to go and contain the danger, and if it wasn't Ryan it would be another of the fire crew, so which one was more expendable if it were all to go wrong?

None of them! I can't lose any more people.

Ryan was a father. To a little girl who had already lost her mother. She didn't need to lose her dad too. And that was all this was, right? Concern for a little girl she'd never met?

But she had no time to think more deeply about it, because she needed to do a primary survey on this driver, trapped right in front of her. He had a large laceration to his scalp, many cuts embedded with glass on his face and hands, and a rapidly expanding forearm with distortion that spoke of a broken bone or two. The arm could wait to be splinted. It was his left arm, and she couldn't reach it from the roadside. But she could get his head bandaged to help control the blood loss whilst she performed her primary survey.

'Chrissie, can you get this?'

Chrissie, the paramedic with her and one of her team mates from the pub quiz, nodded and got to work.

Addy used her stethoscope to listen to the man's chest. He sounded a little bradycardic, but there were equal lung sounds, so that was good. She couldn't feel any depressed skull fractures and there was no way to ask the patient where he had pain.

She stood up as Chrissie placed an oxygen mask on the man's face and got the attention of Paolo.

'We need to get this man out as quickly as possible so he can be more fully assessed.'

'On it.'

Paolo got the attention of two of his crew mates and they began to cut open the vehicle after placing a protective blanket over her patient.

It was hard sometimes to stand back and wait. As a paramedic the urge to action was strong, but it was imperative that they do this right. This man's ability to walk and even have a future relied on their knowledge and training to know when it was right to stand back and wait and when to treat. When to go slow and when to act fast.

She looked up briefly, over to the motorhome. Where was Ryan? She couldn't see him, and felt some anxiety, but then he appeared as he came around the back of the vehicle and she felt a palpable sense of relief. Felt a smile appear on her face. Felt some of her tension leave her.

How strange that she should feel this way. And why? She barely knew him.

He kept me safe underground.

That was all it had to be, right? She owed him— that was all. And he'd been kind at the quiz night, even walking her to her car in the dark when she'd decided to go home.

They'd walked quietly, side by side, and she'd felt nervous about saying anything so had kept quiet before pointing her key fob at her car and hearing it unlock.

'Well, this is me,' she'd said.

'Thanks for a great night. And for being so generous about the prize.'

'It was my pleasure.'

And it had been. She'd felt good about offering him the tickets. A little girl would get more out of a zoo experience than she would. A family deserved the ticket and she didn't have one. She was alone, and most probably always would be.

Ryan had leaned in and opened her car door for her, like a gentleman. It had been nice. Thoughtful.

She'd clambered in. Put her key in the ignition.

'Well, goodnight, Ryan. Get home safe.'

'You too.'

And he'd let go of the car door.

She'd closed it, wound down the window.

'See you at work, maybe?'

'And if not Saturday. Ten a.m. At the zoo.'

'I'll meet you there.'

She was kind of looking forward to it. Having someone to go with. Spending some time with him. Him and his daughter. It would be nice. It meant not having to be at home alone, waiting for her next shift, trying to fill the hours with something, anything, so as not to be reminded that the house was so quiet because she was the only one in it.

The driver was out now. On a backboard. Addalyn let one of the other paramedics splint his arm, then assess him and whisk him away, so she could deal with the next trauma. There were a few lacerations. A degloving incident with a motorcyclist, who was sitting on the side of the motorway, cradling his bad hand. He'd worn a helmet and leathers, but not gloves.

'Let me look at that.' She examined him quickly. It would need surgery—that was for sure. She glanced behind her to quickly assess his bike. It was crumpled at the front. 'You ran into someone?' she asked.

'The red car. Threw me over the top.'

'Wait—you were thrown? Sit still.' She clambered behind him and held his head in place, whilst calling out for assistance.

Ryan came running over. 'You okay?'

'This motorcyclist was thrown over a car. He got up and walked over here, but I want him properly assessed in case of shock. Could you fetch me a neck collar and grab a couple more paramedics for me?'

'Sure thing.' And he ran off to do her bidding.

'I'm okay. It's just my hand,' the motorcyclist said. 'Nothing's broken. I just walked.'

'Your legs might be fine, but what about your neck? Your back? You were in a collision.'

'I don't feel anything else wrong but my hand, and even that doesn't hurt much.'

'Because you've not got any nerve-endings left,

that's why. It doesn't mean it's good. And it could be only adrenaline keeping you upright right now.'

'Honestly… I'm fine.'

'What's your name?'

'Miguel. Miguel Aguila.'

'Where's your helmet, Miguel? And don't move your head.'

'I have it.'

One of the women nearby showed it to her. The helmet had significant scuff marks across it that showed Miguel had slid across the road on his head, and there was even a crack. He might have a closed head injury.

'Can you tell me what day it is, Miguel?'

'Friday.'

Correct. 'And who's our king or queen?'

Miguel paused. 'Charles?'

'Are you asking me or telling me?'

'Telling you.'

'Who's the prime minister?'

There was silence. 'I don't know. But I don't follow politics if I can help it.'

'Wise man. What did you eat for lunch?'

'That's easy. I ate…' Miguel's voice trailed off and then Addy's sixth sense kicked in as she felt a shift in Miguel's condition. He slowly began to lose consciousness and keeled over, with her guiding him down as much as she could.

At that moment Ryan arrived with two more

paramedics, Cindy and Emma, pushing a trolley and carrying a head collar.

'LOC just moments ago. Helmet shows evidence of a substantial impact. Let's get him on the trolley. Em, can you get the oxygen on him, please? I'll do the collar.'

Miguel was still breathing. He had simply lost consciousness. The question was, why?

Addy examined his head and felt the shift of bone beneath her fingers in the occipital area. 'Damn. Let's get him blue-lighted immediately.'

As Emma and Cindy whisked Miguel away, Addalyn looked at the frightened onlookers who had gathered at the roadside.

'Has anyone else sustained any injuries at all?'

They shook their heads. They looked as if they were shocked at having been involved in something so momentous, and were hugely relieved to have escaped without significant harm. That tree might have come down on a car roof. Instead it had hit the road, causing the nearest car to swerve immediately, another to hit its brakes and then, like a domino rally, cars had shunted each other, spun each other and, in the case of the transit, flipped over, most probably due to an uneven load in the back.

'You okay?' Ryan asked.

'Of course. You?'

'I'm good.'

'Good.' She gave him a brief smile. 'I'd better

check in with Paolo. See if there's anyone else in need.'

'I think we were lucky. The rest of these people will probably get away with a bit of whiplash.'

'They'll feel it tomorrow.'

'Police have already started mapping out the site, and we're about to do clean-up so we can get the motorway flowing again. Life never stops, does it?' he asked.

'It can do. And for some people life is never the same again.'

Ryan nodded, understanding on his face.

She hadn't meant to be maudlin. Life might continue, but when tragedy struck, those affected often felt in limbo, marvelling at those around them who just seemed to carry on as if nothing significant had happened.

Time had stood still when she'd lost her father and Ricky in one fell swoop. One moment they were alive. Her father. Her brother. Two people who loved her and cared for her. Her inability to have children didn't matter to them. And then they were gone, in an instant, and she was left alone in a hospital waiting room with her father's wedding band in a small plastic bag and her brother's St Christopher medallion in another.

That was all that was left of their presence here on earth—a couple of bits of metal that had sentimental value.

And memories.

And the knowledge that she would never get to speak to them again.

What had been their last words to one another? She couldn't recall.

'I'll see you tomorrow.'

Ryan laid a hand on her arm and rested it there for just long enough before he disappeared for her to register how reassured and comforted his touch made her feel.

Acknowledged. Seen. Appreciated.

Yes. But also liked and cared for.

His touch had surprised her. Pleased her. Made her yearn for more.

She felt a little bereft when he ran back to help his crew, and she admired his form as he did so. He didn't shirk the gruelling work. He mucked in with his team to help clear the road of debris.

He's a good guy.

But she knew she couldn't get involved with him. And that tomorrow she would have to be careful. Keep her distance. Maybe focus on Carys? Make sure the little girl had a good day out?

Then she wouldn't have to worry about having any little moments with Ryan.

Seems good to me.

CHAPTER FOUR

Carys had wanted to wear a pretty dress so that Addalyn would like her.

'*She's going to like you no matter what you wear,*' Ryan had told her that morning before they drove out.

'*I still want to look pretty.*'

'*But you're going to get a zookeeper experience. It might be better for you to wear your jeans and a nice tee shirt instead.*'

But Carys had insisted. And so here they were, waiting by the zoo entrance, with Ryan in jeans and a nice tee shirt and Carys in one of her party frocks—a beautiful pale green dress with soft white polka dots on it. She wore strappy white sandals and had even tried to paint her toenails, he noticed. In bright, bubblegum-pink.

He smiled, having managed to bribe her to wear a cardigan, too, and had bent down to kiss her on the top of her head when he heard a voice.

'Good morning! You must be Carys?'

And he watched as Addalyn knelt to be face to face with Carys and shake her hand, her face full of smiles.

Addalyn had chosen to wear a dress, too. A denim shirt dress, belted at the waist with a bright red belt. And her hair was down for the first time. Waves and waves of black hair that shimmered blue and indigo in the sunlight.

She looked beautiful.

'Hi, Addalyn,' said Carys, smiling. 'Thank you for winning the prize and sharing it with us.'

Ryan smiled. They'd practised that sentence in the car, with him telling his daughter it was a polite thing to say and do.

'Oh, you're very welcome. But you must call me Addy. All my friends do.'

Carys grinned. 'Addy.'

She stood and bestowed a smile upon him that gladdened his heart.

'Shall we go in?' she asked.

He nodded and stepped back, indicating that she should go first.

They entered the zoo and showed their prize ticket at the gate. The girl behind the desk beamed a smile at them and asked them to make their way to the giraffe house, where they would be met by the head keeper in fifteen minutes' time. She handed them a small map, pointed out where they were at the moment and showed them which path to take to find the location they needed.

'Thanks.'

Exiting the entrance building, they stepped out

into sunlight. It was going to be a lovely day. Blue skies. A gentle breeze. Not a cloud to be seen.

'Did you drive here?' he asked Addy.

'No, I took the bus. My car's at the garage, having a service. I drove it there and caught the bus from the stop outside.'

'They didn't offer you a courtesy car?'

'They did, but I don't mind taking the bus.'

Carys had noticed an enclosure coming up on their left and ran over to look at it. As they got closer, they saw it was full of meerkats, and that there was a group of meerkats perched on top of a fallen tree trunk, staring back at the crowds.

'Daddy, can you see them? They're so cute!'

Ryan laughed and nodded, lifting her up onto his hip for a better look. There appeared to be Perspex domes inside the enclosure, so that people could go underneath the ground and pop their heads up and be closer to the meerkats.

'Can we do that, Dad?' asked Carys excitedly.

'Maybe later, honey. We need to get to the giraffe house, remember?'

She nodded and slid back to the ground, looking for the next exciting enclosure and finding it when she saw chimpanzees playing on some ropes. She squealed with excitement.

'She loves animals,' he said, feeling he ought to explain to Addy.

'I do, too. I don't blame her.'

'What's your favourite?' he asked.

'I like tigers.'

'They're Carys's favourites, too.'

'Really? Then she and I are going to get on!'

He laughed, and watched as Addy followed his daughter to the chimpanzee enclosure and stood beside her, helping to point out the animals, watching them play.

Carys was being Carys. Chatty. Sociable. Laughing. Smiling. Talking to Addy as if she'd known her her entire lifetime, even though they'd only known each other for ten minutes. But his daughter was like that. Everyone said so. When she'd started nursery the teachers had said that she was a confident, clever and happy girl, who wasn't afraid to talk to anyone. And when she'd started reception year her teacher had been so impressed with her she'd awarded her a Buddy Badge, which meant that she was the girl anyone could go to if they felt lonely or had no one to talk to. Carys would make them her friend and find them more.

She got that quality from her mother. Angharad had always been a social butterfly, loving life and going to all the parties and events where they'd lived. She loved being with people. Becoming a mother had placed limitations on that, she'd said, when she'd left. It had kept her at home and she hadn't liked how that had made her feel. As if life was passing her by and all she could do was look after a crying, squalling baby that wouldn't settle when she tried to comfort her.

That had been a huge thing in their relationship. Angharad had had difficulty comforting Carys when she was a baby, and yet Ryan would come home, pick up his daughter and she'd stop crying instantly. He'd tried telling Angharad that she just needed to relax. That Carys could pick up on her mother's frustrations and fears. But his wife hadn't liked him telling her that, either.

He'd thought he was helping. He'd just made it worse. Angharad had thought he was criticising her, but he hadn't been. He'd been trying to give her some advice. Trying to help her bond with Carys, because he'd seen how apart from her Angharad was feeling.

It had been strange, because Angharad had loved being pregnant. Had sailed through her pregnancy. Had blossomed, in fact. And yet when Carys was born, his wife had changed. She hadn't been the mother he'd thought she would be.

So it was nice to see Carys interacting so well with Addalyn.

They made their way to the giraffe house and saw a sign for the zookeeper experience participants, telling them to stand by and wait. So they did.

'Have you ever seen a giraffe in real life, Carys?' Addy asked.

'No. They're meant to be really tall. Like really, *really* tall!'

Addy laughed. 'Taller than me?'

'Taller than a house!'

'Taller than a castle?'

'Taller than the moon!' Carys beamed and slipped her hand effortlessly into Addy's.

He watched as a look of pleasant surprise crossed Addy's face, and then a warm, happy smile.

It was nice to see. Very, very nice.

The door opened and a young woman stood there, in a khaki shirt and shorts and boots.

'Hello, everyone! My name is Macy and I'm going to get you to help me feed the giraffes today. So, who's going to be my special helper?'

'Me, me, me!' said Carys, her hand in the air, practically bouncing up and down on the spot.

'And what's your name?'

'Carys.'

'Well, Carys, that's a very pretty dress you've got on. We won't want to get it dirty, so we'll have to be extra-careful. Why don't you and your mum and dad follow me?'

Addy glanced at him when Macy said *'mum and dad'*, but Ryan simply shrugged and let the assumption stay. What did it matter if it was wrong? What would be the point in explaining to Macy? It didn't matter. Not really. It was nice, actually. Because he'd never had that. That feeling of being a complete family unit. And if he wanted to pretend for a bit, then why not? Who was it harming? Carys certainly seemed happy about it, and was holding on to Addy as if she never wanted to let go.

They climbed some metal steps, their shoes clanking, and came out onto a platform with a metal safety rail. The aroma of giraffe was pretty strong, and now he understood why. There were three giraffes looking directly at them. At head level! And off to one side was a big pile of leaves and branches.

Macy stood in front of them. 'Giraffes are traditionally found in Africa, and they are the tallest living mammals on the planet. Giraffes are considered to be ruminants. Do you know what that means, Carys?'

His daughter shook her head.

'It means that they're animals that get their food from grazing plants, such as grasses and leaves from trees. They then ferment that food in a special stomach before they can digest it.' Macy turned to scratch the head of one of the giraffes. 'This is Mabel. Next to her is her sister Ethel, and the slightly smaller one is Ethel's daughter, Clara.'

'Can I touch one?' asked Carys, her face filled with wonder.

'Why don't you grab a branch and offer it to one of them? She'll reach for it with her tongue and when she takes the branch you can stroke her.'

Carys chose a branch and held it out and the giraffe called Clara came forward to take it, her long, dark tongue wrapping around the branch to strip it of leaves.

Carys let go of Addy's hand to reach out and stroke the giraffe. 'She's so soft!' she exclaimed.

Macy smiled. 'These are what we call reticulated giraffes. They have quite a distinctive coat pattern with polygon markings. Do you know what polygon means?'

Carys shook her head.

'It means five-sided. If you look at the dark markings on her coat, you'll see each of them is five sided, separated by white fur—do you see?'

Carys nodded, her face awash with wonder and joy.

They all stepped forward with branches to feed the giraffes. Ethel, Mabel and Clara were clearly used to being fed this way by humans. They took a great interest in what was being offered to them and were not afraid to interact with them at all.

'Why do they have horns?' asked Addy.

'Both male and female giraffes have them, but you can tell the sex of a giraffe from their horns. If they are thin, and have tufts of hair, then you're looking at a female giraffe. If they're bald, then it's a male. They use them in combat, when they're fighting over food sources or females.'

'Oh...'

It was fun to feed the giraffes. They were quite gentle, with wide brown eyes and long, black tongues that they used almost like a tool.

'We have seven giraffes here in Tutbury Zoo, but Clara will be leaving us soon to become part of a new breeding pair down in Devon.'

'Won't she be sad without her mummy?' asked Carys.

Ryan felt his heart ache when he heard her ask the question. She often asked him what mummies were like, and why she didn't have one, and although he'd tried to answer her questions as truthfully as he could, they often made him feel he was failing her somehow.

How did you tell your own daughter that her mummy had felt tied down by being a mother? That she'd lost her freedom? That looking after a child who cried all the time had made Angharad feel that she wasn't cut out to be a mother? It would make Carys feel it was her fault, when it totally wasn't! Angharad's leaving had all been about Angharad, but Carys wouldn't see it that way.

And so he did his best. Told Carys that her mummy hadn't been able to stay. That some people thought they could be parents, but then found out that they just couldn't.

'She might be a little scared,' said Macy now. 'Especially with the travelling down to Devon. But then she'll be excited to be somewhere new, and to meet different giraffes and make a new family of her own.'

He could see that Carys was sceptical about this.

Addy crouched beside her. 'I'm sure her mummy will be sad to see her go, but that's what happens when you grow up sometimes. You move out and make a family of your own. I'm sure you'll do it one day.'

'And Daddy will be sad when I leave?'

Addy nodded. 'But you'll still be able to see him and you might not even move very far away.'

'What if I don't want to make a new family of my own?'

'Then that's absolutely fine, too. There's nothing in this world that says you have to. Lots of people don't have children.'

He looked at her then, and wondered. Addy was in her mid-thirties, if he had to guess, and she didn't have any kids. Was that a choice she'd made? He didn't want to ask.

But she seemed to like kids. Or she seemed to like Carys, anyhow.

'You can stay with me however long you like,' he said, to reassure his daughter.

Carys turned and smiled at him.

'Do you want to help me let them out into the main yard?' Macy asked.

Carys nodded.

'Okay. Follow me.'

They followed Macy back down the steps to a series of gates and levers. Macy showed Carys which lever to pull to open up the giraffes' enclosure to the outside yard. His daughter took a hold of the lever and pulled it down, and as she did so the metal doors slid open, revealing the zoo outside and the outdoor giraffe enclosure, and Ethel, Mabel and Clara turned to look, before slowly heading out.

'Okay! Now I'm going to take you over to the ape house, where I believe you're all going to help prepare their food and clean the house.'

'Are we going to see tigers today?' asked Carys.

'That's the last step on the tour,' said Macy.

'You like tigers, too?' Addy asked Carys.

'I *love* tigers!'

'Me too!'

'Yay!' Carys threw her arms around Addy and gave her a big hug.

Addy hugged her back, squeezing her tight, and Ryan couldn't help it. He felt great about how the two of them were getting on. He'd known it was going to be good, but he'd not imagined the two of them would click so well. Addy was giving his daughter her full attention. Listening to her. Interacting with her. Holding her hand as they walked and pointing out interesting things. Clearly Addy was having a great time, too.

At the ape house they went into a kitchen area where there were huge piles of produce waiting to be prepped. They spent a good half an hour chopping fruit, leaves, seeds, bark and eggs, and then mixed it with some special monkey pellets which looked like small biscuits. The keeper added an insect mix afterwards.

'We like to try and reflect what they might eat in the wild,' he said.

'I thought monkeys only ate bananas,' said Carys.

The keeper, Ian, nodded. 'Lots of people think that. They do eat fruit—as you can see here—but we don't give them too much of it. We've found that by reducing fruit we can improve an ape's dental health as well as their physical fitness. Fruit that has been commercially grown for human consumption is different to the fruit available to primates in the wild, so we're very careful with the amount they consume.'

Carys looked lost.

'They're just trying to keep the monkeys healthy,' said Ryan, realising that Ian might not know how to simplify some of the terms he used so that younger kids could follow. Perhaps he was new?

'Oh, okay… Like Miss Roberts tells me not to eat too many sweets?'

Miss Roberts was the family dentist.

'Exactly!'

'And the fruit here is like sweeties for the monkeys?'

'That's right.'

'Oh…'

They headed out into an empty enclosure and Ian told them that they should all try to hide the food around the compound as it would 'enrich the apes' living experience'.

Again, Ryan had to explain. 'It's like a game for them...so they don't get bored.'

Carys had great fun stuffing food inside a rubber tyre. She even climbed a rope onto a platform and balanced half a watermelon on a pole there. Addy held her arms out to help Carys down. Once they were done, they were able to go out to the viewing area and watch as Ian released some orangutans out into the open for them to go and forage.

'Look, Addy! They found my food!'

'They did! Aren't they clever?'

Ryan started taking pictures on his phone. Carys was pointing at the apes. Addy was kneeling down next to Carys, with her arm around her shoulder. He took one of Addy and Carys laughing so hard and so genuinely it almost looked like a mother and daughter photo. He stared at the photo, his heart captured by the sheer joy on their faces.

Was this what Carys needed? A connection with a mother figure? She certainly seemed to be enjoying it. Revelling in it, actually. And Addalyn seemed genuinely happy, too.

He looked up from his phone at the two of them, deciding to put his phone away and enjoy this moment with them. Stepping forward, he laid a hand on Carys's back and pointed at a mother orangutan with her fluffy-haired baby.

'Aww! They're so cute!' squealed Carys.

'Having fun?' he asked Addy.

'I really am. I wasn't sure how this was going to go, but I am loving it. Carys is great, you know?'

'Thanks. I think so, too, but I am biased.'

'It must be difficult, raising her alone and having to work, too?'

'It's been a juggling act, but it's easier now that she's at school full time.' He looked at her carefully, before he said, 'I love being a dad. And you're great with kids. You're clearly a natural.'

She smiled at his comment. 'Thanks.'

But she looked a little sad. He was going to ask her if she was all right, but she spoke before he could.

'Hey, Carys, have you seen that one up at the top of the platform? He's huge!'

Clearly she wanted to change the subject, which was fine. The subject of whether people wanted children or not could be tricky to navigate. You couldn't assume that every woman wanted to have a child. You couldn't know if someone had had problems trying to conceive. It wasn't a conversation that you just blundered into, and he didn't want to upset Addy. They were all having a good day.

They fed the penguins next, actually getting to go into the enclosure with buckets of tiny nutrient-rich fish that were loaded with vitamins. The keepers made them wear overalls and boots and gloves, so that afterwards they wouldn't smell of fish, and it was great fun feeding them, watching them dive into the water or waddle on land. They were quite noisy too!

After that they went into the elephant house and helped to give the elephants a bath, spraying them with water from hoses after using what looked like a garden broom to give them a scrub.

The two elephants they were working with—Achilles and Bindu—loved their baths and playfully squirted water over themselves and their keepers, and in turn Addy, Ryan and Carys! They tried to stay as dry as they could, but it didn't really matter because they were all having so much fun! After the elephants' baths they were able to hand-feed them, and Bindu in particular was most enamoured with Carys, using his trunk to constantly sniff the little girl, making Carys giggle continuously at his antics.

And then came the moment that he knew Carys and Addy had waited for and looked forward to the most. The big cats. There wouldn't be the chance for any personal interaction, but they were given a behind-the-scenes tour and were able to help clean out a couple of pens.

'This is Sierra. She's a Sumatran tiger—a species which is critically endangered. But we are very proud to say that she is expecting two cubs, and has only about another month before she delivers.'

'She's going to be a mummy?' Carys asked in awe and wonder.

'That's right,' said Sally, the keeper. 'Sumatran tigers are usually smaller in size than the other tigers you might know about, and can you see those white spots on the backs of her ears?'

They all nodded.

'They act as false eyes and make other animals think that they have been spotted from behind.'

'Nature's so clever!' said Addy.

'Their coats are unique to each animal, so when Sierra has her two cubs they will each have their own pattern. Sumatran tigers usually have stripes that are closer together and more orange and black than other tigers'. They also have webbed paws, which makes them very good swimmers.'

'It's not true that cats don't like water, is it?' asked Carys.

'That's definitely not true! Sierra loves sitting or bathing in her pond out in her enclosure.'

'Where's the daddy?'

'The father is Loki, but you can't see him today, because he's currently with the vet, having a dental procedure.'

'Does he need a filling?'

Sally smiled at Carys. 'Kind of. He broke a tooth and developed a little abscess. It's being cleaned out, so it doesn't make him ill. We try to keep high levels of good health for our animals as we want them all to survive and work within our breeding programme.'

'She looks so majestic,' said Addy, gazing at the tiger as she panted away on her bed.

'She is a beauty,' agreed Sally.

The tiger wasn't the only beautiful creature he could see, Ryan thought.

'Tigers are meant to hunt and kill other animals to survive, so…what do you feed them?' asked Carys.

'You're absolutely right. Tigers do like to hunt—usually at night—so we feed them a variety of meat that we hide in their enclosure, so they have to hunt for it, or climb, or work out how to get the meat that's hanging from the trees.'

Sally knelt down and looked his daughter right in the eyes.

'Have you ever touched a tiger tooth?' she asked.

Carys shook her head.

'Want to see one?'

'Yes, please!'

Sally pulled a real-life tiger fang from her pocket and handed it to Carys. 'This came from a male Amur tiger called Colossus. Do you know where Amur tigers live?'

'No…' Carys took the tooth and gazed at it in wonder.

'They come from Russia. They used to be called Siberian tigers.'

'I've heard of those! I've seen them on the telly.'

'You have? Then do you know how many are left?'

Carys looked sad. 'Not many.'

'That's why tigers such as Sierra are precious. We not only try to keep up their numbers here in captivity, we also work around the world helping to educate people about tigers, their habitats, and how we humans can help them survive in the wild.'

'How can we?'

'Well, we work with the communities near tigers. The people there help us watch them and count them. And because the locals take an active part in monitoring them, it helps us reduce poaching. Do you know what poaching is?'

Carys shrugged.

'It's when someone illegally hunts an animal and kills it.'

'Oh. That's bad...'

'It is.'

'Why do people kill tigers?'

'That's a very good question. Some people want their fur. Others believe that parts of the tiger can be used in medicine.'

'Can it?'

Sally shook her head.

'I want to help a tiger. How can I?'

The keeper smiled. 'You're so sweet to want to help. We offer adoptions here, where you can adopt any animal in the zoo. Or you can get your mum and dad to help you look online and see if there's an animal charity you want to support instead.'

Sally was the second person to mistake them for a family. The idea that he and Addy were married, was... Well, Ryan could see the flush on her cheeks, too.

'I'll think about it.'

Sally smiled. 'Good idea. You don't want to rush into anything. I think you're a very wise little girl.'

'I'm going to be a vet when I'm older.'

'Sounds perfect for you. Now, let me show you the ocelots.'

They had a great time looking around the zoo, learning a lot about all the animals, and when the morning was over they headed to Reservation, the zoo's restaurant.

The restaurant was very elegant. Soft grey decor, crisp white tablecloths and hyper-realistic animal art in graphite pencil all over the walls. It was like a mural of a jungle, lit by wall sconces and candlelight. Greenery cascaded down from multitudes of baskets above their heads, and the soft scent of hibiscus was barely there.

Ryan, Addy and Carys were seated at a table in a bay window that overlooked the flamingo enclosure. Lots of salmon-pink birds stood in the water, occasionally dipping their beaks to try and feed on whatever it was flamingos fed on.

Ryan would bet Carys knew what they ate.

'What are you going to have, Carys? Do you need any help with reading the menu?' Addy asked.

She was sitting next to his daughter and opposite him.

'What's this?' Carys pointed to the menu.

'Vegetable lasagne.'

'Oh, I love lasagne! Can I have that?'

'Sure,' said Ryan. 'What do you fancy, Addy?'

'I don't know. Having seen all those animals, I'm kind of glad that this restaurant doesn't serve any animal products at all. I'd feel weird eating them after that.'

'I agree. All of this sounds lovely, but I'm not sure what to pick.'

'I think I might start with the gazpacho...'

'I'll join you. What about a main course?'

'Erm... I think maybe the vegetable chana with pilau rice?'

'Hmm... I think I'll go for the Brazilian black bean chilli.'

They gave their choices to the waitress, who took their menus from them and then provided Carys with a tablet to play animal games on whilst she waited.

'This is so nice... I can't remember the last time I sat in a restaurant,' Addalyn said.

'Really?'

'Really. I think the last time was before I lost Dad and Ricky.'

'What was the occasion?'

Addy frowned.

'Why were you in a restaurant?'

'Oh! Hen night for a group of friends.'

'You don't have a significant other who takes you out for a meal? Just the two of you?'

'There was Nathan... But that was so long ago I can't even remember.'

'Nathan?'

'My ex. Obviously. We did go out to restaurants in the early days, but then our lives became so consumed with other stuff I guess we forgot to remember we were actually a couple.'

He could understand that. When he and Angharad had first met, everything had been wonderful. A whirlwind of romance and nights out on the town. But then, after they'd been together for a while, living together, then married, work had become a priority for him—especially after he'd begun to feel that he was failing her as a husband. Angharad had never seemed happy. No matter what he'd tried. And then she'd got pregnant with Carys.

Yes, it had been unplanned, but she'd seemed to love being pregnant, and he'd thought, briefly, that everything would be all right between them again. But it hadn't worked out.

'Life can get like that, sometimes,' he said.

'Maybe. But I often blame myself.'

'Why?'

She glanced at Carys, but his daughter was absorbed in a game where she could chase butterflies with a net.

'Maybe I neglected him.'

'Did he tell you he felt neglected?'

'No. Not directly. But eventually his actions spoke louder than any words he might have used.'

Ryan frowned, unsure what she meant.

'He met someone else,' she said in a low voice, looking awkward.

Oh. He hadn't meant to make her feel bad. Because they'd been having a lovely time here today and the day wasn't over yet! The obvious hurt in her eyes pained him.

'I'm sorry. I didn't mean to pry.'

She shrugged. 'It's fine.'

'No, it's not. You must have been hurt.'

Were those tears he could see forming in her eyes? He had tissues in his pocket. He always carried them. For Carys. But now he passed one to her and felt his heart soften at the way she thankfully took it and dabbed at her eyes.

'A little.'

He wanted to reach for her hand. To comfort her. But he felt that he couldn't with Carys right there next to them. He didn't want to confuse his daughter with what was going on between them. He'd already told her that they were just friends who happened to work together, and that was all.

Instead, he tried to show it on his face. With

his concern for her. His apology. 'I know what it's like to lose someone you once loved. To have them walk away and choose somebody or something else other than you.'

Addy gazed back at him. And then at Carys. She nodded.

CHAPTER FIVE

SHE DIDN'T WANT to talk about Nathan. She'd closed that episode in her life long ago. One huge painful episode, locked away in a box. She'd once believed it would be the only painful episode in her life, and then she'd lost Dad and Ricky, further breaking her heart...

Now she had lots of pain locked away in the dark recesses of her soul, and she never intended to examine it again. She was trying to reclaim her enjoyment of life. Find meaning in her work. Saving lives. Keeping people safe. Giving other people a future. It gave her some meaning. A reason for being here.

She intended to find her life's purpose in serving others, because that was all she could foresee. Stealing moments for herself that she would savour in private and hope that it would be enough.

But today? So far she was loving her time with Ryan and Carys. Carys was the sweetest little girl. Enthusiastic, warm, clever. And best of all Carys had kept on holding her hand, wherever they'd been that morning. They'd shared some lovely moments feeding the animals, and washing the elephants had been so funny. Especially when that one elephant had trumpeted water everywhere. They'd got a little wet, but Addy hadn't minded at all. Her dress had dried quickly in the lovely sunshine and so had Carys's.

They'd all been laughing, especially Ryan, and just for a moment…for one brief second…she had allowed herself to imagine they were her family. That Ryan was her boyfriend or her husband, just the way Sally and the other keeper had clearly thought. That Carys was her daughter and that this was what love and family would look like. What it would *feel* like.

When had she last truly laughed like that? When had she last truly *belonged*?

And then that brief moment of joy had been followed by such a long, extended moment of hollow grief, in which she'd known that she was just borrowing someone else's family. That she was pretending and that none of this belonged to her. What was she doing? Believing in it? If she believed in it and enjoyed it too much, it would just make going home alone even harder than it normally was.

The tigers had perked her up somewhat. Getting so close to such magnificent animals. To Sierra, who was carrying the hope of two new precious lives.

Was she jealous of a tiger?

Having a baby had once been her entire reason

for being. Having Nathan's baby was all she'd ever wanted at one time in her life…

'I only lost a boyfriend. It must have been harder for you. Losing not only your partner, but the mother of your child,' she replied.

'It was a shock, yes, but that doesn't mean my pain was greater than yours. Everyone deals with pain, grief and loss in different ways. What could bring one person to their knees might not even upset another.'

'I guess…' She looked at Carys, still absorbed in her game. 'What was she like as a baby?'

'I have pictures.' Ryan got out his phone and scrolled back through a photo album before passing the phone to her. 'Just keep swiping left.'

Her fingers brushed his as he passed the phone, and she felt a frisson of something race up her arm and smack her squarely in the gut. Trying vainly to ignore it, she began to scroll through and saw the first picture was of Carys as a baby, being held by her mother, Angharad, in the hospital. Angharad looked tired, but happy. There was a BP cuff around her upper arm, a cannula in the back of her left hand.

Angharad was pretty. The kind of woman who didn't need make-up. She had long, luxurious hair. Honey-blonde. Elegant hands and long thin fingers and she wore a doozy of an engagement ring. It must have cost a fortune. Carys was scrunched up, tiny, with chubby fists and a shock of dark, fluffy hair. She looked perfect. They both did.

'She's beautiful.'

'She was eight pounds two ounces of perfection,' Ryan said with a smile at his daughter.

Addy loved the way he looked at Carys then. Full of love and adoration.

'Was she a good baby?'

She scrolled through many more pictures. One of Ryan holding Carys. One of the three of them together, as if a midwife had taken the photo for them, or maybe a visiting friend or family member. Carys swaddled in her cot at home. Carys having a bath. Carys crying as water was poured over her head to wash her fluffy hair. One of her lying on a changing mat. And then a swathe of professional baby shots, all artfully done in black and white as Carys slept. Swaddled within a circle of daisies. In a basket. On a pretend cloud...

And then there was a shot that almost stopped her swiping. Made her want to peruse the image a little more closely. Another black and white arty shot. Ryan and Carys. But Ryan had no top on. He was doing skin to skin, cradling his daughter, and all she could see apart from a perfect baby was a perfect guy. Muscled and fit, with flat abs and a small military tattoo on his upper arm.

She wanted to study him. Absorb him. But she also didn't want to be caught staring at him, so she swiped on and began to notice that Angharad was in hardly any of the photos now, and when she was she looked distant, as if she weren't truly present in the moment.

Did Angharad not know what a gift she'd truly been given with this perfect baby and wonderful man? How had she walked away from all of that?

'She was very good. The kind of well-behaved baby that makes you think you've cracked parenting and could easily have another.'

'You wanted another?'

'Of course I did! I always wanted lots of kids.'

Another reason she could not have him. Because she could never give him what he wanted.

'Wanted? Past tense?'

He shrugged. 'I *do* want more kids. Being a dad is the greatest thing in the whole world. But finding the right person who wants that too is hard.'

'I guess…'

'Plus, it's going to take a lot of time, you know? Meeting someone that's right for you. Meeting someone that's not only right for me, but someone who's also right for Carys. I mean, I don't think I've ever asked her if she would want to have a baby brother or sister one day.'

'I want a sister,' Carys said, having clearly been listening.

Addy smiled and glanced up at Ryan. 'See? You have your answer.'

He grinned. 'Maybe one day, honey.'

'If I get a sister, that means I also get a mummy, right?'

'That's true—though technically she'd be your step-mum,' Ryan answered.

'Ooh. Would I help choose her?'

'Er...actually, yes, I think you will help me. When that day comes.' Ryan managed to look a little uncomfortable.

'I'll help you too,' said Addy, leaning in towards Carys. 'It's going to take a strong woman to take on a fireman.'

'Why?'

'Because a fireman has a dangerous job and that can put a lot of strain on a relationship. It's got to be someone who will go into it knowing she could get a phone call at any time to tell her that her husband has been in an accident and is hurt.'

She didn't want to say *or worse*.

'Does that mean that I'm strong?' Carys asked.

Addalyn nodded. 'It does. You're very strong.'

'Cool. Then maybe I could teach my new mummy how to be like me.' Carys pressed 'play' on her game again and became absorbed, as Addy looked up at Ryan and smiled.

'You see? It's easy.'

'Is it?'

Ryan raised an eyebrow as the waitress arrived at their table with their starters—gazpacho for both Ryan and Addy and a small green salad with croutons for Carys.

The food was delicious, and after such a busy morning they'd worked up quite an appetite. The gazpacho was sweet and refreshing, a little peppery, and gone much too soon. But then their main courses arrived and Addalyn tucked into her chili hungrily.

'I wonder what we'll be doing this afternoon?' said Carys.

'I think we're free to roam around the zoo on our own now,' said Addy. 'Anything you want to see in particular?'

'I don't mind. How about you, Daddy?'

Ryan shrugged. 'I'm happy to just see where the path takes us. So, Addy, what do you normally do on your time off from work?'

The question surprised her, and she wasn't sure how to answer.

This and that... I stay out of the house as much as I can... I waste time sitting in cafés or bookshops...

'I guess it depends. Erm... I like going and looking around bookshops. I...er...do a little dressmaking on occasion.'

'Really?'

'Yes. I made what I'm wearing now.'

'You made that?'

She blushed as his gaze swept over her body. Clearly he was looking at her handiwork, the dress, but it felt as if he was looking at her body.

'Is it difficult?'

Her mouth was dry. 'It can be, sometimes. But I've been doing it for so long now I kind of know what to do.'

'Well, I think that's pretty amazing. I tried to make an outfit for Carys's Christmas show once. She was an angel, so all I had to do was sew a sheet and tie her waist with some tinsel, but I couldn't even do that.' He laughed.

'Maybe Addy could help you make my Halloween costume!' Carys piped up eagerly.

'What's this?'

Ryan groaned. 'Oh, she's been on at me to make her the costume of one of her favourite book characters. No one seems to sell it, as it's a little obscure, but I've told her I'll do my best.'

'What's the character?'

Addy was interested. It might be fun to make something for Carys, and it would give her something to do when she had to be at home. Plus, as a bonus, she would have to keep seeing Carys for fittings, and that meant also seeing Ryan. Whom she liked. A lot. Despite his being a fireman and totally on her list of forbidden things.

'She's a princess,' said Carys.

Addy frowned. 'That doesn't sound too hard.'

'And...?' urged Ryan, raising his eyebrows at his daughter.

'And the captain of a space fleet. Her name's Hattie.'

'A princess space captain? Hmm... Does this book of yours have pictures?'

Carys nodded.

'Then you'll have to show me, so I can get some sort of idea.'

'Okay!' Carys seemed thrilled.

'You don't have to. It's going to be a lot of work,' said Ryan, obviously trying to give her a way out.

'It's no problem. I'd be happy to help out. I've got, like, six weeks? That should be plenty of time to work around shifts and school.'

'Carys? Say thank you to Addy.'

'Thank you, Addy!' Carys threw her arms around Addy and gave her a big squeeze.

Addy laughed and hugged her back. 'You're very welcome.'

Seriously... Was there anything better than this?

Their second to last stop was the gorilla enclosure. Addy wanted to see the big silverback and there he was, in all his magnificent, muscled glory. Sitting in the middle of the enclosure, with his back against a tree, he surveyed his group of females and their babies. There were one or two juveniles playing around, swinging from ropes and tyres and chasing each other, but most of them were basically just enjoying the September sunshine.

The crowds were thick around this enclosure, watching from up high, looking down at the gorillas below. Plenty of people were taking pictures of the big silverback, especially when he opened his mouth to yawn and revealed an impressive set of sharp, dangerous-looking fangs. He was a proud beast, and Addy was impressed by his presence. The way he just seemed to know he was the most important of all and that he owned all that he surveyed. It was his territory, through and through, and no intruders were going to come after his near and dear ones.

Which made it so incredibly shocking when someone in the crowd suddenly screamed, off to the left. Addy looked to see what was going on and realised someone had fallen.

A child had fallen into the enclosure.

Instantly she whipped her head back to check on the silverback. He was already up and slowly making his way across the grass as his females scattered with their babies and ran to the other side of the enclosure, away from the child.

The child's mother was screaming, yelling, trying to distract the big silverback, and so was everyone else.

Addy looked at Ryan. Hoping her gaze told him everything.

We need to move. We need to help.

'Carys? Come with us.'

They began to run away from the enclosure, pushing through the crowds that had begun to gather to see what all the commotion was about.

'He's going to kill him!' Addy heard someone

scream, and she hoped that it wasn't true. That they wouldn't be too late.

They burst into the welcome centre and Addy grabbed a woman from behind the desk. 'Please look after her!' She knelt in front of Carys. 'Your daddy and I have some work to do, okay? We'll be back. I promise. Just stay with this lady.'

Carys nodded, looking frightened.

Addy saw a rush of employees heading to a door marked *Staff Only* and followed them, with Ryan close behind. Once through, they found a room with a bank of screens overlooking the situation. The silverback was just sitting there, only once lifting his hand to prod at the small child that lay motionless beside him on the grass.

Addy and Ryan identified themselves to the staff.

'We have the Dangerous Animal Response Team formulating a plan now,' they were told.

'And how long will that take?' asked Addy. 'You need to disperse the crowd around the enclosure, because all the screaming and noise could cause that silverback to react badly.'

'Thank you, but we know what we're doing.'

'Do you? Because I don't see anyone trying to control the situation. You need to disperse the crowd and then either tranquilise the silverback or see if he can be called back to his indoor enclosure. Will he do that?'

One of the men looked at her. 'Maybe. If we got Garrett to do it.'

'Where's Garrett?' asked Ryan.

'I'm Garrett.' A young man with a straggly beard stepped forward. 'Kitaana seems to like me.'

'We need to get all the gorillas out of there so we can attend to that child. Have you called for an ambulance?'

'Yes, of course we have.'

'Then you need to get those gorillas out of there. Get the females inside with the babies—that might bring Kitaana in, yes?'

'It might be safer to dart him,' said another zoo employee. 'It's policy if the public become endangered.'

'Get the dart ready, but let's try the other way first. There's no reason Kitaana should suffer because a member of the public made an error.'

They moved quickly, and Addy watched the staff as they began opening up the doors that would allow the gorillas to return to their inside enclosures. The females ran in quickly, holding their babies and looking panicked. Addy could see that they were frightened by this event, too, not understanding what had happened. They were used to being watched by the public. To having humans nearby every single day. But they'd never come up close to one who wasn't a keeper. They'd never come into contact with people whose faces and scents they didn't know.

And now one was with them, lying motionless on their grass.

'Kitaana! Hey, boy!'

Addy and Ryan stood behind the tempered glass, watching as Garrett tried to get the silverback away from the boy.

The boy still lay face-down on the grass, with Kitaana beside him. The silverback had made no aggressive moves at all.

Kitaana looked to Garrett, then back at the boy.

'Bedtime, Kitaana. Come on, now!'

The silverback looked around his enclosure. He saw that the rest of his group had gone inside and slowly stood up, leaning over the boy. He made a low rumbling noise, and then slowly began to walk towards the enclosure doors.

Addy felt a surge of relief that this seemed to be working, and that no further harm would be done to the boy by the gorilla, but that still didn't mean it was over. The boy had suffered a significant fall and might have all manner of injuries. He did look as if he was breathing, but that was all they knew about his condition.

'That's it, Kitaana. Good boy. That's it…'

The silverback entered his enclosure and Garrett slid the door shut. As soon as it was closed Addy grabbed the basic first aid kit that was kept next to it and, with Ryan, ran out into the gorilla enclosure.

It felt weird, knowing that moments ago a huge,

powerful animal had been present but that they were now safe. Rule one in any emergency was that before you ran into an accident site yourself, you checked that it was safe to do so.

'Get the rest of these people away—it's not a spectator sport!' Ryan ordered the staff as he followed her into the enclosure.

Addy settled herself beside the boy, glancing up briefly and meeting the gaze of the boy's mother before giving the boy a visual assessment. He had some cuts and grazes, and his left leg looked longer than the right, which suggested either a fracture or a dislocation. His right arm was bent in a way it shouldn't be, and she had no idea if he had any broken ribs puncturing organs inside. He could be bleeding internally. Every second was precious.

'What's his name?' she called out to the mother, up above.

'Leo!'

'Okay. Leo? Can you hear me? You're okay. We've got you. But if you can hear me, I need you to open your eyes. Can you do that for me?'

Leo's eyelids flickered, but didn't fully open.

So he was near consciousness. Maybe…

She ran her hands over him, checking his skull for any visible signs of deformity, feeling for the tell-tale signs of a possible skull fracture. Leo was unconscious, but he wasn't vomiting, and there was no bleeding from his nose or ears. There was no bruising behind his ears or beneath his eyes, so maybe he was just concussed? No one would know for sure unless he had a CT scan of his head, which wouldn't happen until he was in hospital.

Addy checked his neck. Ideally, she needed a cervical collar, but there wasn't one in the first aid kit and they were still waiting for the paramedics to arrive. His airway was clear, and without equipment she was reluctant to move him.

Leo groaned and began to cry. A good sign. In fact, it was a relief. Leo looked to be about five, maybe six years old. Skinny, though, so not much padding. When he'd fallen, he would have fallen hard.

'What should we do?' Ryan asked.

'Nothing until the paramedics get here with a collar and board. They'll get him on oxygen and insert an IV. Let's just keep him talking and awake, and be ready to roll him if he stops breathing.'

'You think he will?'

She shook her head. 'Children are strong. Resilient. And they can compensate for their injuries a lot longer than adults can. Leo? Sweetheart? My name's Addalyn and I'm a paramedic. This is Ryan and he's a fireman. You've had a fall, and I know you must be hurting, but try to stay still for me, all right? That's very important.'

Leo nodded his head.

'Don't move, sweetie. Don't nod your head. Just say yes or no, okay?'

'Okay…' Leo sounded incredibly frightened.

'Don't worry. We're going to look after you and you're safe. There are no animals here. All the gorillas are inside. It's just us and we're waiting for the ambulance to arrive.'

As if on cue, the sound of sirens could be heard as Addy finished speaking.

She looked at Ryan with relief. It was at times such as these that she realised just how much she depended on the equipment she usually had with her. She had nothing right now except for the few bandages and antiseptic wipes that existed in the first aid kit. It was designed for basic cuts and scrapes, not catastrophic falls. But having Ryan by her side was calming.

'They're nearly here. Tell me, Leo, what's your favourite animal?'

'G-G-Gorillas.'

She smiled. 'Well, the gorillas that you were with looked after you when you fell. They didn't hurt you. They were just curious. Even the big fella. The silverback. He sat with you and watched over you until we got here, so I want you to keep them as your favourite animal, okay?'

'O-Okay.'

'Good lad.' She stroked the side of his face gently, trying to provide comfort, keeping him talking until the arrival of the paramedics.

Apparently, he didn't like football, so couldn't tell her his favourite team. He preferred playing tennis. His favourite colour was blue, and his favourite ice cream flavour was triple chocolate chip.

She recognised the paramedics when they came running into the enclosure. Mikey and Jones. Good guys. Addy explained what had happened, and the results of her primary survey. She watched as together they splinted Leo's arm and leg, then gave him some painkillers, IV fluids, an oxygen mask and a collar, before they carefully, with perfect choreography, manoeuvred Leo onto a backboard. He cried out as they moved him, so they upped the painkiller before they got him on the trolley and wheeled him to the ambulance.

His mother was running alongside, crying and apologising as she went.

'I was filming the gorilla! I didn't see Leo climbing over the barrier to get a better look! I didn't see! I'm so sorry!'

Addy said nothing. She could feel the mother's distress and understood her position. You couldn't watch a child twenty-four-seven, and who wouldn't want to capture the perfect picture of that magnificent silverback? But at the same time she was meant to be responsible for her child. Her maternal guilt would beat her up about this incident more than anyone else could. Something like this would make the evening news, or at least the local newspaper, and plenty of people would have judgments to make. This mother did not need Addy's judgment. She and Ryan had simply been there to help.

With the ambulance gone, they were thanked by the zoo staff for their assistance and offered tea and coffee, which they turned down. They wanted to get back to Carys, who had to be frightened by events.

When they went to find her they found her in the staff room, munching on a biscuit and playing with someone's phone.

'Daddy!' She ran to her father and Ryan gave her a big squeeze. 'Is that little boy okay?'

'He will be, honey. He's at the hospital now, getting all the help he needs.'

Carys smiled, then looked up at Addy. 'Did you put him back together again? That's what Daddy says you do.'

'He was still in one piece, thankfully. I didn't have to do much mending.'

She didn't need to tell Carys about all the possible injuries Leo might have. Why frighten her?

'So, can we go home now?'

Addy looked at Ryan and he nodded.

'I think we've all had enough adventure for today.'

Ryan got Carys fastened into her car seat, then checked and double-checked the seatbelt before he stood up and closed the car door. Addy was standing there, waiting to say goodbye.

'Well, it's certainly been a day to remember,' she said, with a glorious smile.

'It certainly has. Can we give you a lift home?'

'I can take the bus.'

'Let me give you a lift. I know Carys would like it.'

Addy looked uncertain, but then she smiled again. 'Well, if Carys would like it…okay, then.'

She began to open the rear door.

'You can sit up front with me.'

'It's okay. I'd like to sit with Carys. Make sure she's okay.'

'All right.'

He got into the driving seat and started the engine, glancing into the rear-view mirror to check that Addy was seat-belted up. He couldn't help but notice the way Carys leant into Addy, looping her arm through hers and resting her head against Addy's arm. And he also couldn't help but notice the way Addy smiled. Her face was full of contentment and joy as she laid her head against Carys's.

The two of them had clearly bonded, and he wondered if he had held Carys's happiness back by not letting any women into their lives. He'd thought he was doing a good thing, not having a string of women coming and going through their lives. He'd certainly not been ready. He'd been afraid of how it might make his daughter feel, but also of how it might make him feel.

When he'd stood in that church and sworn to spend his life with Angharad he'd meant it. And he'd fought for his marriage. Fought to keep Angharad with them. His daughter had needed her mother. He'd wanted his wife. When she'd walked away, leaving them behind, he'd never felt pain like it. But he'd had to push it aside to look after Carys. There'd been no time for him to collapse, to wallow in depression. He had a daughter. And she'd needed her daddy more than ever now that she didn't have a mother.

The idea of letting another woman into his life when he'd so clearly failed with Angharad had left him doubting himself. Left him worrying about just what he had to offer a partner. He wasn't simple. He came with baggage. A child whom another woman would have to take on if their relationship ever got serious.

He'd often thought, even though Carys was confident and outgoing, that maybe she'd be different with a mummy figure—but look at her!

'Everything okay?' Addy asked, having caught him staring at them.

'Just thinking about how happy you both look.'

Addy smiled. 'She makes it easy. You must be very proud that you have such a wonderful little girl. You're doing a good job.'

'You think so?' He felt a warmth in his chest. Her words made him feel good. 'I often have my doubts.'

'Don't.'

He gave her a nod and then began to pull out of the car parking space. 'So, the big question is… where do you live?'

'Union Road. You know it?'

He raised his eyebrows. 'I do. It's two streets over from us.'

'Is it? Which road are you?'

'Thatcher Lane.'

'I know it well.'

'I can't believe we live so close to you.'

'Did you move into that small house on the corner?' she asked. 'The one with the large hydrangea bush in the front garden?'

'That's the one!'

Addy laughed. 'Wow. Okay…'

'Does that mean I can come round to your house and play?' Carys asked.

'Carys! You don't invite yourself to people's houses. You wait to be invited,' Ryan interrupted.

Addy raised a hand in protest. 'That's okay. I'd love you to come round one day. I don't have any toys or anything, though.'

'That's okay. I can bring mine. What do you like to play?'

'I don't know.'

'Do you like jigsaw puzzles?'

'I love jigsaws! I haven't done one in such a long time, though. I might not be any good.'

'That's okay. I can help you. Daddy has just bought me a five-hundred-piece one with tigers on it. I think it's going to be hard, but it would be fun to do together.'

'Okay! You're on.'

Ryan smiled and pulled out into the traffic. 'Beware, though...five hundred pieces...might take some time.'

Addy nodded and laughed. 'Sounds perfect. How about next weekend? Saturday?'

Carys beamed.

'She won't forget,' he warned Addy, with a smile.

'Neither will I,' said Addy, hugging the little girl once more.

It had been such a long time since he'd felt so content. Since he'd felt he was with someone to whom he could trust his heart. He could, couldn't he? He was wary of rushing into anything. And he didn't want to get hurt again. But the way Addy was holding on to Carys and enjoying her company reminded him of what he'd thought it might have been like if everything had worked out with Angharad. He'd hoped for these moments. Wished for them. Imagined them. And now he could see it in a woman with whom he worked. A woman who was not Angharad.

Was he ready to face these feelings? This overload of emotions?

One last glance in the rear-view mirror showed him that Carys had her eyes closed. Was she falling asleep? Snuggled into Addy like that? Most times he didn't mind her falling asleep in the car. He'd simply carry her out at the other end and place her in her bed. But they'd be dropping Addalyn off first.

'Which number Union Road?' he asked quietly.

'Four.'

'Okay.'

She gave him such a smile then, and it did even more crazy things to his insides. Today had been incredible. Crazy and scary at times, but he'd face any gorilla, any day, rather than have to figure out how Addalyn was making him feel.

Because what if this was serious?

He felt as if he was on a precipice and about to fall.

Did she feel the same way? He wasn't sure she did, because she looked so secure in herself. So happy. So content. Maybe he was reading too much into this? Maybe this was just a fun day for her? She'd bonded more with Carys than she had with him, and apart from her beautiful smiles he'd not noticed her sending him any signals.

I'm wrong. I have to be.

CHAPTER SIX

THE CAR RIDE came to an end much too soon, and before Addy knew it Ryan was pulling up outside of her house.

It seemed to stare at her knowingly. Taunting her.

When you come back in you're going to be alone. All alone! Again!

Her day with Ryan and Carys was at an end. Her unexpected day. Her gift from the win at the Castle and Crow. And what a wonderful day it had been. Apart from the little boy, Leo, falling into that enclosure, the day had been wonderful and dreamy. Just the sort of day she would have imagined for herself if she'd ever been so lucky as to have created a family of her own.

It was so easy to imagine Ryan as her partner. So easy to imagine Carys as her daughter.

But they couldn't be.

Ryan was a firefighter, and she simply would not attach herself to another man who put his life at risk every day. She'd worried enough about her dad and Ricky and rightfully so, losing them both in one fell swoop in that building collapse. She could not be with Ryan and go through that kind of worry again.

Besides, he'd told her today that ideally he wanted more children, and she couldn't give him that. It hadn't worked with Nathan, and Nathan had left her, finding himself a woman who could give him the children he'd so desperately wanted.

And Carys? She wasn't her daughter. And she couldn't deny that precious little girl the chance to have a brother or sister. But she could pretend, at least for a day, that she was her mother.

'Here we are,' Ryan said, coming to a halt outside her property and pulling on the handbrake.

Addy glanced at the house one more time. She could envisage its empty rooms. Its quietness. The living space with its empty chairs. Dad's empty spot. Ricky's. Their faces smiling down at her from the photos she had framed and lined up on the mantelpiece, to keep them with her as much as she could. The neat, tidy kitchen, without the crumbs that her dad would leave behind every time he made himself a cheese sandwich. Without the knife perched over the edge of the sink in case he decided to make himself another. The empty bedrooms. The wardrobes still filled with their clothes. Clothes that, on occasion, she would still press her face into, to inhale their scent that was fading now.

Time was slowly erasing all evidence of them

and only her memories remained. Memories that could quite often be haunting.

'Thank you for giving me a lift.'

'You said your car's having a service?'

'Yes. It should be ready on Monday.'

'Need a lift to pick it up?'

'You're very kind, but I can walk it.'

Addy looked down at Carys, still slumped against her, fast asleep. She didn't want to wake her. Didn't want to move her at all. If she could stay here for the rest of her life in this bubble, pretending, then she would. Very happily.

'She looks so content. I don't want to disturb her,' she said quietly, stroking Carys's hair.

'She'll be okay.'

Addy nodded, trying to draw out the moment, but knowing she shouldn't. So, she leant down and kissed the top of Carys's head.

'Hey, sleepyhead. I've got to go.'

Carys mumbled and stirred, but didn't wake up as Addy moved away and undid her seatbelt. Every movement was torture, because she knew every movement was a return to her loneliness. Her solitude. It was probably a good thing that Carys didn't wake up, because it would have made it so hard to say goodbye. Even though they did have a jigsaw date next weekend.

Addy opened the car door and got out, closing it behind her gently, but firmly. Still the little girl didn't stir.

Ryan got out too. 'Nice house!'

She turned to look at it, forcing a smile. 'It's all right. I'll give you a tour when Carys brings over her jigsaw.'

'You know you don't have to honour that promise, right? A five-hundred-piece jigsaw? That's not something that gets completed in one visit.'

'I don't mind. She can come over as often as she wants. I like her. I like her a lot. And it's not a hardship to spend time in her company.'

'What about spending time in mine?' he asked.

Addy looked at him, her heart pounding in her ears. How to answer? Should she tell him the truth? That she liked him enormously? That she found him attractive? That she longed for more? For human contact? To be loved? But that he terrified her all at the same time?

'You're okay. Not as great as Carys, but…' She laughed.

Ryan laughed too. 'Of course not. Who is?'

'Honestly, it's fine. Besides, I made her a promise and I don't break my promises to children.'

Ryan nodded appreciatively. 'You're amazing. You know that, right?'

Addy laughed nervously. 'Thanks. Erm…so are you.'

For a moment they just continued to stare at one another. The air in the gap between them was taut as a bow, and neither of them seemed to know what to say or do next.

Would he step forward and drop a kiss on her cheek?

Would he step away and simply say goodbye, giving her a cheery wave?

Which would she prefer? The heat and excitement and danger of the kiss? Or the disappointment of him simply walking away from her? If he kissed her, what would it mean? A simple friendly thank-you? Or something more?

If he walked away that would mean he didn't see her as anything other than a colleague or a friend. And somehow, in that moment anyway, she really didn't want to be just a colleague or a friend, no matter what job he had. She wanted the excitement and danger of a kiss on the cheek. She wanted the wonder. She wanted the thrill.

She wanted to be seen and acknowledged.

'Well, I guess I'd better go...'

'Yes.'

'Thank you for today. It was an adventure.'

She nodded. 'It was.'

'You're back at work on Monday?'

'Yes.'

'Me too.'

'Great. Maybe I'll see you?'

'Yes. If not, what time would you want me to bring Carys around next Saturday?'

'Around eleven? I could do lunch, and then we can jigsaw in the afternoon?'

'Sounds great.'

'Great.'

Another moment of tension, and then suddenly he stepped forward, placed his hands on her upper arms and leaned in to drop a kiss to her cheek.

She sucked in a breath and closed her eyes, trying to absorb every exciting moment as his lips brushed against the side of her face. He was close enough for her to hold. To touch. To kiss back if only she turned and faced him.

But she wasn't brave enough.

Because she was much too scared to let this become something else.

To let Ryan become something else.

And then he was stepping away, walking back to the driver's side of the car, and Addy looked down and saw Carys looking at them both.

She was smiling.

CHAPTER SEVEN

'Is ADDY YOUR girlfriend now?' Carys asked as he got into the car.

Carys had tricked them both. Making them both think that she was asleep. Or had she just been fortunate and woken to see her father kiss a woman?

He was so bamboozled by the question that he just laughed awkwardly and shook his head. 'No, of course not! We're just friends. That's what you do when you say goodbye to friends. You give them a quick hug or a kiss goodbye.'

'I don't say goodbye to my friends like that.'

'No? Well, that's because you're little. You will when you're older.'

'Why?'

'I don't know. You just do.'

He started the engine and glanced out of his window at Addalyn. She wasn't going in, but was standing there, waiting for him to drive away. To wave goodbye.

Kissing her goodbye had felt good. He'd dithered about doing it. About how to leave her. Not sure what they were. But at the core of his feelings was the fact that after today they were definitely good friends, and so he'd chosen to do what he always did with his female friends—politely kissed her cheek, thank her for her time and walk away.

Only it hadn't worked that way with Addy. It hadn't felt as casual as that. He'd sensed in her a yearning for a connection. As if she was a solitary castaway on an island who needed the comfort of another person, loaded with need. Her eyes had said it all, almost like she didn't want him to go.

The softness of her skin, her alluring scent and the sensual caress of her long dark hair as he'd pressed his lips to her cheek had sent his senses into overdrive. His mind had gone blank. He'd almost forgotten what he was doing...had allowed himself to pause as he breathed her in... And just before he'd pulled back slightly, tempted by the idea of a full-on kiss—one his daughter wouldn't witness because she was asleep, so maybe it would be okay—his logic and higher reasoning had jumped in to protect him and he'd stepped away completely.

I'm not ready. I might not be good enough for her. What if she doesn't feel that way?

And now he was back in the car with a curious daughter and he had to drive away.

Why isn't she going inside her house?

Addy continued to stand by her front gate, watching them drive away, one hand raised in a wave. From this distance she looked like a ghost, with her pale face and dark hair. He felt drawn to keep looking at her, to keep wondering. And then he knew he couldn't do it any more, so he took a turning he didn't need, just so he didn't have to keep looking back. To keep regretting. To keep being annoyed at himself for being so cowardly.

When she was out of sight he still didn't relax, feeling he would have handled himself better if given a second chance.

'Daddy?'

'Yes, baby?'

'Are you okay?'

He pulled over and stopped the car to turn and look at her. She'd never asked him that question before.

'I'm fine.'

'You look sad.'

He tried to laugh it off. 'I'm not sad.'

'Are you lonely? Madison, at school, she only has a mummy and no daddy, and she says that her mummy gets sad sometimes because she's on her own.'

'I'm not on my own. I have you. You're my everything. I don't need anybody else.'

Carys smiled. 'But don't you sometimes wish? Because sometimes I wish for a mummy.'

Her words touched his heart. 'I know you do. And sure... We all wish sometimes.'

'I like Addy.'

'I do, too.'

* * *

The house felt so empty when she went inside. Quiet. Much too quiet. Devoid of life and warmth and joy. She dropped her bag by the bottom of the staircase and with a heavy sigh made her way out to the back garden, unlocking the French doors and swinging them wide, so that she could stay outside for just a moment longer and breathe freely. She felt stifled inside. The warmth of the day had made the house seem fusty on her return.

Addy gazed at the trees, their branches softly moving in the gentle breeze. At the flowers turned up to the fading sun. At next door's cat, George, perched on the fence.

Life was beautiful. It could be beautiful. But why did she only allow herself to enjoy it when she was with others? Why did she insist on beating herself up about coming back to this place? Would it be best if she moved?

No. Their memories are here. If I moved away, I'd feel like I was losing them all over again.

Addy knew she needed to find a way to deal with her solitude. To find a way to enjoy being in this house again. Perhaps she needed to decorate it? Make it more her own now that it was no longer her father's?

She turned to look back into the kitchen. It hadn't been updated or remodelled for at least a decade. Maybe if she breathed new life into it, she might feel better? If she worked on the house as much as she was trying to work on herself maybe that would make her feel better about being here?

She stepped back inside and walked through the kitchen to the lounge. She looked at the wall-paper on the feature wall. It was a soft mushroom colour, with a tree effect on it. It looked a little sad, but maybe she could change that? She went over and looked at it. Down at the bottom, a piece was curling free. She took hold of it in her fingers and gave it a big rip, tearing a huge strip away.

And she felt a real buzz of excitement, and a rush...as if more and more of the past was being ripped away.

A fire had broken out in a small marina. Originally a cooking fire, on one barge, the flames had spread to three other boats and now the thick black smoke billowed up into the sky.

Addy saw it as she raced towards the scene in her rapid response vehicle. There were two known casualties, suffering burns and smoke inhalation, but she had no idea if there were others.

On the scene, she quickly appraised the casualties and handed them over to the paramedics when they arrived. They'd get them to the local burns unit quickly. Then she began a conversation with the fire chief, Paolo. Blue Watch were on duty, which meant that maybe Ryan was here, too.

'What have we got?' she asked.

'Pan burning on the hob on this boat.' He pointed

at the burnt-out shell. 'Left by the first female casualty, who is suspected to have dementia. The second female casualty had left her for a moment, to deal with a mechanical issue down below. The fire then spread to boat two, where we think it rapidly burnt its way up the sail and mast, which collapsed onto boats three and four, causing considerable damage.'

'Any other casualties?'

'My crew are sweeping the boats now.'

'Any hazardous materials?'

'Gas canisters. Boat fuel. The usual. All have been secured.'

'Have we established a perimeter?'

'Got the boys in blue on it.'

'Good. Keep me apprised.'

'Will do.'

She wanted to ask him if Ryan was one of the firemen she could see fighting back the flames. The blaze was furiously eating up the old wooden barges. This marina in particular, she knew, was an historic one, where tourists came to view the older boats that sometimes took people out on tours around the local canals. She'd been on one of them herself, with Dad and Ricky, and enjoyed it so much, she'd taken Nathan. But he'd hated what he called 'the faff' of the locks and the slow progress of everything. He'd hated that it took almost a day's sailing to get somewhere that would take fifteen minutes in a car.

She watched the firefighters as they slowly covered the flames with water and foam, making their way forward slowly but surely. A sudden bang had her flinching and cowering in shock, her arm raised to cover her face, her heart in her mouth. When she turned around, she saw that something they'd overlooked must have exploded in the heat. The firefighters all looked to be safe, though, and were continuing their push forward.

Her heart thudded painfully in her chest. It simply reminded her of the call with her dad and Ricky. Watching helplessly, unable to do anything. Worrying about the two men whom she loved so deeply and hoping that they would be okay.

What if the firefighters had been closer to that explosion? What if they'd been blown into the water? What if, God forbid, they'd been hurt? What if one of them had been Ryan?

She could easily ask Paolo who he had fighting the blaze. Could easily check. But she refused to do so. Because asking would mean something, wouldn't it? If she asked him it would reveal, not only to herself but to everyone else, that she cared about Ryan in particular. And she could not admit that to herself, never mind anyone else.

So she stood there and waited, biting her lip and keeping her torturous thoughts to herself.

With the blaze finally contained, Ryan pulled off his helmet and ran his hands through his sweaty hair as he made his way across the marina towards Paolo and, behind him, Addalyn.

'It's under control now, boss.'

'No further casualties?'

'Thankfully, no. Looks like all the boats were empty, as they usually are at this time of day.'

'Good. Finish off and then let's clear the area.'

'Will do.'

He peered past Paolo as his boss stalked down the grassy verge towards the carnage, and smiled at Addalyn.

'Hey.'

'Hey.'

She smiled back at him. A shy kind of smile. A sweet smile. One that seemed to say she was mightily relieved to see he was okay.

'How have you been?' he asked.

She paused for a moment. 'Good. You?'

'Yeah. A bit hot, but I'm okay.'

He pulled off a glove and examined his wrist. He'd felt that blast when it had gone off. He'd been incredibly close. But adrenaline had kept him going. Until now. Now he could feel hurt and pain, and he wondered if he'd been caught by something.

Instantly she was by his side. 'Let me look at that.'

She took his arm in her gentle, delicate hands, turning his wrist this way, then that. 'Can you feel me touch you here? And here?'

'Yes. It's sore, though. It's not a burn, is it?'

'No, it looks like something hit you when that blast went off. Did you feel anything?'

'Not in the moment.'

'You should get it properly looked at. You have good range of movement, but there are so many little bones in the wrist... You might have fractured one.'

'I'll get it checked.'

'I can splint it for you in the meantime.'

'No, that's okay.'

He had to pull his arm free. It was distracting him. Her touch. The way she held him.

It had been a long time since someone had taken care of him. When he'd married Angharad she hadn't taken any interest in his injuries. If it wasn't gushing blood, or broken, then she didn't get alarmed or worried. And she hadn't thought he should. He wasn't a dainty snowflake. He was a strong guy who worked out. Who looked after himself. He had to, working for the fire service.

And all the scrapes he'd got into in the army meant he didn't worry about the little things either. Army medics in particular didn't mollycoddle you. They patched you up and sent you back out if it wasn't anything deadly serious.

But to see the concern in Addy's gaze now, the intensity of her examination and the soft way she touched him, as if she really cared about him, was disturbing.

'You need to get it checked, Ryan.'

'I will.'

'When?'

'Later.'

'You can't work with a broken wrist. You could jeopardise a rescue if it decided to give out on you during a shout.'

She was right. And he hated it that she was right.

'I'll report it to Paolo as a possible injury,' she insisted, but she was smiling, trying to show him that she was only doing this for him so that he didn't get into trouble, and not just because she wanted to be a thorn in his side.

He laughed. 'Okay, okay... Thank you for checking it out.'

'You're welcome. Are you still coming on Saturday with Carys? I thought I could get the measurements for her Halloween costume whilst she's there.'

'Sure. But only if you're still happy to do that?'

'Of course! Why wouldn't I be?'

He had no way to answer. Because he was very happy to go and spend time with her. He knew Carys would be happy, too. But it felt like something scary.

I mean, what am I doing? What am I pursuing here? A friendship? Something more?

He'd always known that someday there might be someone else. In fact, he'd hoped for it, not wanting the rest of his days to be spent in solitude once Carys moved out and started a family of her own.

But this soon?

His head was a mess. His logic was confused. The only thing that was perfectly clear was how attracted he felt to Addalyn Snow.

It took Addy four days to complete her renovation of the living room.

The old wallpaper had come off easily with a steamer. She'd sanded the walls and filled in the cracks, then bought new wallpaper in a soft duck-egg-blue and applied it to the walls after watching a few how-to videos online. It turned out she had quite a knack for wallpapering.

Next, she'd repainted, covering her doors and skirting boards in a fresh coat of glossy white paint and her ceiling in a matt white. Yesterday a new pair of curtains had arrived in the post, and she'd taken down her father's old brown ones and put up her own to match the wallpaper. She'd re-arranged a few photo frames, added candlesticks, put a new rug over the wooden floors and added some potted ferns she'd bought from the local garden centre and now the living space felt fully transformed.

She was happy with it, and proud to show it off when Carys and Ryan arrived.

'This is what you've been working on?' Ryan asked as he came in and admired her work.

'Yes. Just this room so far. Next, I plan to work on the bedrooms.'

'I can't believe you did all this in one week.'

'It's amazing what you can do when you put your mind to it,' she replied, not wishing to add it was also amazing what could be achieved when you had nothing else in your life and no one to help you procrastinate.

'Well, it looks fabulous.'

'Thank you.'

It felt strange to be proud of the house. For a long time she'd only felt haunted by it. Burdened. Now she was looking at it in a different light, and she had to admit she was already beginning to feel a little better about being here, with all her plans to modernise and make the house work *for* her instead of against her.

'So, what can I get the two of you to drink?'

'Whatever you're having is fine,' Ryan said.

'Could I have juice?' asked Carys.

'Sure. What kind? I have apple or orange and mango.'

'Orange and mango, please.'

'No problem. I'll just get that for you. Why don't you get the jigsaw set up on that table over there and I'll be right back in.'

Addy headed into the kitchen and Ryan followed.

'She's been driving me crazy all week, going on about today. She couldn't wait to come here and be with you again,' Ryan said, leaning against a counter, smiling.

And him? Had he been waiting to be with her again?

His casual presence here with her felt strangely exciting. She grabbed two mugs from the cupboard and began to make tea, before she grabbed a glass and filled it with juice from the fridge.

'I've been looking forward to it, too,' she said.

'There's not many people who'd look forward to spending time with an excitable five-year-old.'

'Well, then, there must be something wrong with the rest of them. Besides, Carys is great, so it's not like it's any hardship on my part. And kids in general are fun! They remind you of what life was like before you had any grown-up responsibilities.'

'Life certainly is easier when you're a kid.'

'Exactly! The world hasn't hurt you yet, or tainted your vision of life.'

Ryan nodded. 'It does do that… I'm not exactly sure if I remember being a kid all that much.'

'You don't? I do. My dad and Ricky were my whole world growing up. My brother and I used to play in this area of green belt land, making dens and bows and arrows, or paddling in the brook trying to catch sticklebacks, or making rope swings on the trees. When I think back all I remember is an endless summer...' She paused. 'With maybe one heavy snowfall.'

'Snowball fights? Making snowmen?' He smiled.

She nodded, her memories reminding her of happier times. Times when she'd felt surrounded by love. Never alone. Even without a mother she had never felt that something was missing, because her dad and Ricky had made sure that she didn't. They'd involved her with everything. Made huge deals of her birthday and Christmas.

In fact, the only time she'd wished she could have a mother had been when her periods had begun and she'd been scared. But, again, her dad had come to the rescue, sitting her down, providing her with the products she needed, explaining everything. Not once had she felt embarrassed about it. Plus, she'd had her friends at school...

But she'd ached for her mother at that point. Realising that all those other important milestones she might have as a woman—puberty, marriage, pregnancy, giving birth—would pass by without her mother at her side.

When she'd struggled with her fertility with Nathan, undergoing all that IVF, she'd wondered what it might have been like to have faced it with her mother to talk to.

That was why she identified so closely with Carys. Wanted to spend time with her. Because she knew, deep in her heart, that even if Carys didn't say anything to her father, maybe she missed her mother anyway. Maybe not too much yet, but as she approached puberty she would. No doubt about it. She'd grown up without a mother by her side and she knew how it felt. And Carys had no brother to carry her through it. Just her dad. Another fireman. And who knew if that spelt doom for her as it had for Addy?

'We made the best snowman, Ricky and me. We went full out. Borrowed one of Dad's hats, one of our grandad's old pipes. Stick arms. Carrot nose. Scarf!'

Ryan laughed.

'Has Carys ever made a snowman?'

'I don't think it's snowed enough yet. But one day we will. Maybe I'll take her skiing one year, or to Lapland at Christmas. Who knows?'

'You should do that. Before she gets too old to want to build snowmen.'

'Does anyone ever get too old to want to build snowmen?'

Addy thought about it and laughed. 'Probably not.'

She'd never been skiing. Or to Lapland. She'd dreamed, with Nathan, that when she got pregnant—when they finally had a baby—they would do all the fun things. Lapland for Christmas. America for all the theme parks. The Caribbean for the beaches. They would explore and have fun and live life after all the rounds of drugs and injections and procedures she'd had and being made to feel like their lives were not their own, but something owned by the fertility specialists who'd kept her on strict regimens.

Maybe they shouldn't have waited? Maybe if they'd had more fun together then Nathan wouldn't have left?

'How strong do you like your tea?'

'I don't mind.'

'Okay. Strong it is, then.'

She passed him his cup and poured some juice for Carys, eager to get back into the next room and spend some time with her.

They walked through into the living area and spotted Carys at the table, patiently holding on to her box.

'So, what is this jigsaw, then?' Addy slid into the seat opposite her and Ryan sat beside his daughter.

'The tiger one!'

'Oh, wow.'

It was a very pretty jigsaw. Three tigers, lying together among lots of brown savannah grass. The pieces were all going to look the same...this was going to be a challenge.

'You don't pick easy ones, do you?'

'If it was easy then we'd finish it too fast,' Carys said.

'Well, we wouldn't want that to happen,' laughed Ryan.

Carys opened the box and spilled out the pieces onto the table.

'Shall we pick out edges and corners first? Try and build the outline?'

'Let's do it.'

They began sorting the pieces. It was a slow process and took them a good half an hour, even with three of them, as occasionally someone would miss one and throw an edge into the middle pile, from where it had to be retrieved and found by someone else. But eventually they'd sorted them all and began constructing the edges.

Addy couldn't help but notice Ryan's hands. His fine fingers. Occasionally they reached for the same piece and would laugh, embarrassed.

'I can't remember the last time I did a jigsaw,' Addy said. 'When *do* adults stop playing games?' she mused.

'I'm not sure all of them do.'

She laughed. 'No. I guess not. But I meant like this. Board games. Jigsaw puzzles. Video games. Whatever it is they loved as a child, when do they drift away from all that and why?'

'I guess other pressures step in. Work. Bills. Socialising. Relationships.'

'Maybe…'

'Do you have a boyfriend?' Carys suddenly asked Addy, stopping to look up at her with a smile.

'Do I…? Erm…well…no, I don't,' she answered, feeling her cheeks fill with colour.

'Do you want one?'

Addy laughed nervously. 'Well, maybe one day.

I did have one, but things didn't work out, so I'm taking care that whoever I choose next is the right one.'

'What was wrong with the last one?'

'Carys, we don't ask our friends questions like that,' said Ryan, trying to give her an out.

But Addy wanted to answer. She didn't want to evade the little girl's questions. Felt it was vital to be as honest with her as she could.

'Well, Nathan and I were happy for a while, but then we had a falling out.'

'When I fell out with Ruby, our teacher Mrs Graves said we had to shake hands and make up.'

Addy smiled. 'Mrs Graves sounds like a very sensible person. But adult relationships can be a lot more complicated than that.'

'Why?'

'They just are. You'll discover that as you get older.'

'So you didn't shake hands and say sorry to one another?'

Addy shook her head. 'No.'

'Oh.'

She looked at Ryan and he gave her a look back that said *sorry.* He had nothing to apologise for. And she did feel she'd answered Carys truthfully, so that was good.

Soon Carys found the last corner piece, and then they were able to attach two longer edge strips to form a bigger corner. The jigsaw was going well, and now they were beginning to find pieces to work on the tigers' faces.

'Here's a piece of fang!' Carys said, with a huge smile.

'Anyone want another drink?' Addy asked, grateful for Carys being there, distracting her, keeping her focused, so that she didn't have to worry about being alone with Ryan.

'I'm fine. But maybe we should stretch our legs for a bit? Go for a walk?' Ryan suggested.

Addy looked to Carys, to see what she thought of that idea. A walk with Ryan would be wonderful! Alone, it would be risky. Too intimate. But with Carys there…? Easier.

'Okay!' said Carys.

It was beautiful out. Sunny, but not very warm. Lots of people were out, to take advantage of the late summer they seemed to be having as September wore on.

'When we get back to the house, Carys, I'll take your measurements and show you some of the fabric I have. You can pick what you want for your Halloween costume.'

'You must let me know how much it costs, though. You're not doing this for free,' Ryan said.

'Nonsense! It's a pleasure.'

'Pleasure or not, I know fabric isn't cheap. I'll pay for what you use.'

She smiled, knowing he wouldn't win that one. She had had no intention of taking payment for making Carys's costume. It was going to be fun. Something she would enjoy doing. Something for someone else. It would give her a purpose.

'I don't want to be that space princess any more,' Carys said.

'You don't? What do you want to be?'

'I want to be a tiger.'

'Oh. Well, I'm not sure I have any tiger fabric...'

'Let's go and buy some, then,' said Ryan. 'I'll pay.'

Decision made, they headed through the park towards the row of shops on the road that led towards the town centre. Halfway down was a fabric and haberdashery shop that Addalyn often used. When they walked in, it was busy, but Carys's face lit up at the sight of all the pretty fabrics on show.

'Ooh, Addy! Look at this one!'

Carys had lifted a corner of soft tulle, delicately embroidered with dainty flowers in pale blues, pinks and mint-greens.

'Gorgeous!'

Addy pulled out a longer strip of the fabric to look at the pattern and see how it repeated. Ideas were whirling in her head as to what she might use it for.

'You won't look like a tiger in that,' Ryan said.

Carys nodded and looked around for animal prints, spotting some at the far end of the shop. They made their way there.

'Now, do you want a cotton print, or fleece, or

fur?' asked Addy. 'Bearing in mind that when you wear this it will be the end of October, so it could be cold.'

Carys was touching all the fabric, but seemed most enamoured by the fur.

'This one! It's nice and soft.'

'Hmm…'

Addy tested it with her fingers to see if the many layers might be too much for her sewing machine to deal with. But it seemed light and thin enough not to be a problem, yet thick enough to keep Carys warm. And if it wasn't, then Carys could always wear some clothes beneath it.

'This could work.'

'How much will you need?' Ryan asked.

'Two metres? To be on the safe side. And— Ooh, what about this?' Addy pointed at some lace trim that she knew would work well as teeth.

'Get whatever you need.'

The lady who owned the shop wound out two metres of fabric and half a metre of trim, folded it all and placed it in a bag for them as Ryan got out his card and paid.

They headed back outside.

'Where to next?' asked Ryan.

'Can we see if my magazine is in the shop?' Carys asked.

Addy looked to Ryan. 'Magazine?'

'She gets this partwork… It's about all the birds

in the world. I think she's got about twelve issues. At the moment they're doing birds of the UK.'

'You like birds?' she asked his daughter.

'Yes! I do! My favourite is the robin redbreast.'

'They are sweet. They're pretty tame, you know? You can get them to feed out of your hand if you're patient enough.'

'Can you?'

This piece of information seemed to blow Carys's mind.

Laughing, Addy allowed Carys to slip her hand into hers and they headed over to the newsagent to see if they had Carys's magazine. They did, so they bought it and headed back towards the park.

'You know, I've got a few bits and pieces in,' said Addy. 'We could easily make up a small picnic in the back garden.'

'Oh, we wouldn't want to put you out.'

'You wouldn't be! It would be a pleasure,' she said, smiling, hoping Ryan would say yes.

She didn't know what it was. She knew she ought to be not getting as involved with them as she was. But she simply couldn't help it. She loved their company. Loved the way it felt to be with them. Loved the way she felt she was a part of something. And she didn't want it to end now that they were here.

At home, they did a bit more on the jigsaw and then, when they'd all begun to feel that they truly couldn't see any of the pieces any more, and progress began to be severely stunted, Addalyn went into the kitchen and began making sandwiches and putting little snacky things like sausage rolls and cocktail sausages in the oven to warm through.

'Please don't go to too much trouble. Carys and I will be happy with a sandwich.'

'It's no trouble. In fact, I like it! It's been such a long time since I got to take care of anybody.'

Ryan looked at her for a moment, then turned around to check to see where Carys was. The little girl was giving the jigsaw one last attempt.

'You miss your dad? And your brother?'

'More than words can say,' she said, feeling a wave of sadness creep over her.

'Do you want to talk about them?'

She did. And maybe he would understand? Being a fireman himself...

'You must have heard what happened to them?'

'I know there was a building collapse.'

Addy nodded. 'They got called to a fire in a block of flats. Twenty floors that needed evacuation due to what turned out to be a faulty electric bike charger. Someone had been trying to charge their battery overnight, but the item was faulty and it started the blaze. We didn't know that until after...'

She paused in her chopping of the strawberries she was working her way through and turned to face him.

'I was there too, helping co-ordinate resources

and the rescue with Paolo, who was newly in charge of Blue Watch.'

'My chief Paolo?'

She nodded. 'He'd worked hard to get his promotion. Had earned it. He and my dad were best friends, and though they'd both gone for the post my dad couldn't have been prouder that his friend got it.'

'He sounds like a good guy.'

'He was the best. Ricky and Dad were tasked with trying to get as many people out as they could. They were using the stairwells, because they were concrete and weren't burning, and for a while it was working. They rescued forty-one people that night, before the heat and the fire became too much. The fire grew out of control, despite their measures to contain and dampen it. Dad and Ricky were in flat twenty-three when a roof gave way and trapped them both. Ricky's leg was trapped beneath some masonry and Dad attempted to pull him out. But then the top of the building began to collapse and they got trapped in the rubble. They burned to death before anyone could rescue them.'

Ryan stared at her in silence. 'You watched it happen? You were there?'

She nodded, wiping a silent tear from her eye. 'I was.'

Suddenly he moved from his spot opposite her and embraced her, holding her tight. It was sudden and unexpected, and she forgot to breathe for a moment, so shocked was she to be in his arms and to be held. But then she let go of the breath she was holding and relaxed into him. She squeezed him back and just allowed herself to be comforted. Breathing in his unique, wonderful scent.

Ryan felt so good. So strong. She could feel the musculature of his body against hers and realised that for the first time in years she felt safe. Protected. Cared for.

It was a heady moment, and one that she didn't want to end.

'Can I have some more juice?' Carys's voice piped up behind them, and suddenly Ryan let her go.

Addy stepped away, wiping her eyes rapidly before turning to smile at Carys. 'Of course you can! Have you got your glass from before?'

She refilled the glass with juice and handed it to her. 'Why don't you go out into the garden with that blanket over there and pick a spot for our picnic?'

'Okay!' But then Carys paused and looked at them both. 'What were you doing?'

Addy froze, not sure how to respond.

Ryan came to the rescue. 'Addy was a little upset. She was telling me about how she lost her dad and her brother. I was comforting her, that's all.'

'Oh. Okay!' And Carys grabbed the blanket and headed out.

Addy looked over at Ryan. 'Thank you.'

'It was the truth.'

'No. For the hug. I hadn't realised just how much I needed that.'

He smiled back at her. 'You're very welcome.'

CHAPTER EIGHT

HE'D HEARD THE story of the loss of Victor and Ricky Snow. How could he not have? He worked in their station. Their pictures and their names and their years of service were up on the memorial wall with the others who had been lost over the decades. But he'd not heard it from her point of view and he hadn't known that she had watched it happen.

He couldn't imagine how that must have felt. To lose a father and a brother at the same time was awful enough, but to be there, helpless, watching it happen, knowing she could do nothing to reach them, must have been an agony he could only hope never to experience. Would he have been able to hold himself together? He wasn't sure of it.

Addalyn Snow was a remarkable woman. Stronger than she knew. And being able to hold her in his arms like that and comfort her had meant more than she knew. He'd longed to hold her. Longed to make her feel better and take away some of her pain. But the feel of her in his arms…the heat of her…her softness… He'd longed to do more. Kiss her. Tell her she was special. Keep her in his embrace and never let go.

Only he couldn't do that.

He helped her carry out the food she'd been preparing and together they assembled their picnic. He felt as if he wanted to give her a reason to smile again. To be happy. Because he felt that he was the one who had reminded her of her sad past and he felt responsible. It had been eye-opening to hear her version of events, that was for sure. And now he wanted her to think of happier times, so he would make her smile.

Losing a crew mate at a rescue was a risk of the job. They all knew that. They all knew the danger, but did it anyway. And they honoured those they'd lost. Honoured their sacrifice in trying to rescue others or to stop a fire from claiming any lives. Lost crew were heroes. Addy's father and her brother were heroes.

'I'm starving!' Carys tucked into a sandwich and opened up a packet of crisps.

'You should try one of these,' Addy said, offering Carys a halloumi stick wrapped in streaky bacon.

'What is it?'

'A special kind of cheese. It doesn't melt when you cook it.'

Carys took a bite. 'Yum!'

Addy laughed.

This was nice, thought Ryan. Sitting in her back

garden, in the sunshine, eating a picnic together. A simple pleasure. This was what it was all about, right? Spending time with family. Enjoying being together.

Addy was going to make someone a wonderful mother one day.

'You ever thought about having kids?' he asked, feeling relaxed and casual.

He felt he could ask her now. They knew each other so much better, and he now knew she'd been in a relationship before, with Nathan, so surely she must have thought about it. Or they must. And he only asked because Addy got on so well with Carys that he couldn't imagine her *not* being a mother.

But he saw a cloud cross her face and realised his error much too late.

'Of course I have. I've always wanted kids. But… I can't have them.'

He stared at her, shocked and surprised.

And feeling guilty. Again.

He should never have pried. 'I'm sorry.'

'It's okay!' she said, clearly trying to say it with a smile. 'I've accepted it.'

'Are you…? I mean, have you seen a doctor about it? Or…?'

'Nathan and I were trying for a long time. We tried naturally, and when nothing happened after a couple of years we went for testing. They couldn't find anything wrong with us, so we began IVF. I had four rounds. Three on the NHS and a fourth that we paid for ourselves, using all our savings. But it didn't work.'

'I'm so sorry.'

'It's not your fault.'

'I know, but... That's twice now I've brought up something sad for you and I'm beginning to feel paranoid.' He tried to laugh it off, to make her feel more comfortable, and he could see that she appreciated that.

'Honestly, it's fine. It's good for me to talk about it. People should talk about infertility openly, so it's seen as natural.'

'I guess...'

'We did have some hope on the second round. I did a home pregnancy test and it was positive, and we were over the moon. But when the clinic did a blood test the HCG levels were so low. Not where they ought to have been. And a second blood test a few days later showed that the levels had dropped even more. So...that was a no-go too.'

'That must have been devastating.'

'It was. All those treatments. The drugs, the injections... You begin to feel like a human experiment, you know? Your life becomes ruled by it all. You can think of nothing else. And as a couple you either turn towards each other after each failure, or you go looking for comfort elsewhere. Like Nathan did.'

'How long have you been apart?'

'Four years now. Four and a half... Something like that. I came back here to live with Ricky and Dad and then I lost them, too. It's been a hard few years.'

'I'm sorry. And I know I keep saying that, but I really mean it.'

'I know. And thank you. It's fine. That's life. Bad stuff happens. We just have to go with it.'

'Of course—but maybe this means that you've had your share of the bad stuff and from now on it's only good stuff all the way.'

Addy smiled and nodded. 'Let's hope!'

They finished their picnic and sat in the sun. Then Addy remembered she had ice creams in the freezer, so they had those. He liked watching her laugh. Loved watching her smile. But more than anything he adored the way she interacted with Carys.

Carys had been his whole world for years, and he would give his life for his daughter. To see Addy loving and having fun with his little girl meant everything.

It made him think about the future. It made him think about what sort of happiness he might find some day. Would it be with Addy? They got on so well together.

But...

He wanted more kids. He always had. And if Addy couldn't have children, then...

There's more than one way to have a family.

Addy looked at him as she laughed with his daughter, and he felt, deep down, that he would be able to pursue those other alternatives if Addy was by his side. Suddenly his heart began to pound as he realised he was thinking about what it would be like to have a family with Addalyn! It scared him. Terrified him. Made him realise that maybe he thought more of Addy than he ought to.

But he simply couldn't tear his eyes away from her as his thoughts raced ahead. Because when he'd held her, comforted her earlier, there'd been a response. He'd felt the way she'd sunk into him. She'd even made a soft sound of gratitude...of affection, and neither of them had really wanted to let go. And she was spending all this time with him. With his daughter. And sometimes he saw a look in her eyes. Of query. Of hope. Of fear.

But mostly he felt she was as attracted to him as he was to her.

Boy, we are both in so much trouble here!

CHAPTER NINE

ADDY RACED THROUGH the streets, sirens blaring, as she navigated the traffic towards her latest shout. An industrial accident… All she knew was that there were a number of workers involved with some sort of chemical spillage.

As she drove, she tried to think of all the things she'd need to be aware of upon entering the site. Getting details from whoever was in charge. Establishing safety protocols. Keeping herself and the other rescuers safe, so that there wouldn't inadvertently be even more casualties than there already were.

It was the number one rule as a first responder—make sure it's safe for *you* before you proceed to assist a casualty.

It was a thought that had been running through her mind a lot just lately. Keeping herself safe. Keeping her heart safe, especially. Because spending time with Ryan and Carys was wonderful and she didn't want anything to spoil it. It had been a long time since she'd felt this happy. And the last few times she'd felt happy life had thrown spanners into the works and ruined everything, taking away the source of her happiness.

Maybe Ryan was right? Maybe it *was* now her turn to have happiness?

She wanted to believe that, but she was scared of not holding back. Not giving her absolute all seemed to be the only defence she had, and if she kept it in the back of her head at all times that she could lose Ryan and Carys at any moment, then maybe she'd be prepared for it, if it ever happened? Just thinking about it even now, as she raced towards someone else's tragedy, made her stomach churn.

She'd only known them such a short time and they already meant so much.

She'd been having dreams of kissing Ryan. A couple of times they'd come close. Both times they said goodbye to each other after spending time together Ryan would kiss her cheek, but she'd been yearning to have him kiss her on the lips.

He had not. Because each time Carys had been there.

At least, she thought that was the reason why. Maybe at the weekend he'd not kissed her on the lips because she'd told him that she couldn't have children. She knew he wanted more. He'd told her that. He probably thought there was no point in pursuing anything with her.

But she dreamed of his lips. Of his mouth. The way it smiled. The way it might feel. All the possible things it could do and how they might feel. And she loved to listen to him talk. He was funny and kind. Empathetic and genuine. That was what she loved about him the most. You got what you saw. He put on no airs or graces. There was no pretence about Ryan. And she liked the way he looked at her. Interested. Content. Warm. He seemed happy in her company and she was very happy in his.

But it was all so difficult, because of what he was—a fireman. Maybe if he was still in the army it would be easier? Or if he was a travelling salesman? Or a postman or a truck driver?

Why did he have to be a fireman?

As she got closer to the location she became aware of more sirens, more blue lights, as other first responders raced towards the scene. It was on an industrial site, and as she weaved her way down the road she became aware of workers in high-vis vests and hard hats exiting the site in an orderly manner, as their own buildings' sirens sounded to indicate that an evacuation needed to take place. Up ahead was a singular fire engine, and behind her came two more.

She felt herself switch into full-on work mode as she searched for a place to park that was safe.

'What are we dealing with?' she asked as she got out of her vehicle, slipping on her own high-vis vest and attracting the attention of what looked like a supervisor from inside the building.

'Acetone production. Somehow a fire started in Block B. We've evacuated, but we're still doing a headcount.'

'Get those numbers to the fire crew as soon as, please. Any casualties?'

'A couple over there. Robert, I think. And Wendy.'

Addy turned to look at two people sitting on a grass verge, both with their hands wrapped in gauze. She used her personal radio to contact ambulance control, update them on the situation and order more ambulance crews. This could be incredibly serious. Then she headed off towards the first fire engine to liaise with Paolo.

'We've got an acetone fire.'

'I've just heard. I've ordered all the men to use their breathing apparatus. Do we have a number?'

'Supervisor is doing a headcount right now. I'm going to check on those two over there and establish a triage tent. Get any casualties brought to me after decontamination procedures, yes?'

They needed to be cleaned of any acetone before they got to Addy as a preventative. To stop any more issues.

Paolo saluted her and ran off to issue orders to his men.

She didn't have time to look for Ryan. Her mind was on her patients.

As she got to their side, she set down her bag

and evaluated them. 'Hi, my name's Addy. Can you tell me what happened?'

She started with questions because they were both conscious and breathing. Robert staring at his hands. Wendy looking away into the distance. A cursory glance told her they did not appear to have any blood-loss or broken bones. They were the walking wounded, and getting them to answer her questions would give her a good idea about their respirations and their ability to talk, and whether she needed to check their airways.

She would do that anyway. It was something always checked after a chemical spill. Some chemicals could burn throats and airways if inhaled, and though her knowledge of acetone itself was sketchy, she did know that high amounts could cause irritation to the mucus membranes.

'We don't know,' said the man, Robert. 'One of the machines had been making funny noises all morning, and we were waiting for Engineering to take a look. We were going to shut it down, but our boss Gregori told us to keep it moving. There was a flash. Sudden. Blinding. And we heard a bang. Next thing we know the room is on fire.'

'You have injuries?' Abby asked, indicating his hands as she slipped on her gloves.

'Burns. My hands hurt like hell, but Wendy says hers feel fine.'

That wasn't good. When burns didn't hurt, it

usually meant that the thickness of the burns was deep and had destroyed the nerve-endings.

'How did the burns happen?'

'We tried to stop the fire. Used the extinguishers. But we got too close. My clothes caught fire and Wendy tried to put me out…rolled me on the floor.'

'And then I slipped and fell into the flames,' said Wendy. 'I think I've burnt my hair too.'

Wendy turned to look at her. All this time she'd been turned away, as if staring off into the distance. She tried to smile. And that was when Addy saw the burns on her face.

Damn.

They went halfway up her face. Reddened and painful-looking. Some of her hair was gone, as were her eyebrows and no doubt her eyelashes. It looked bad enough that she might need a skin graft.

'Did you go through a decontamination procedure?' she asked as she rummaged in her bag to set up for a cannula. She needed to get fluids and painkillers into Wendy immediately.

'I don't think so…'

She couldn't let Wendy or Robert sit there with acetone still burning into their wounds. It might hurt, but she needed to wash the chemical off their skin before she applied new coverings.

Technically, she needed soap and some warm water to wash it off fully, but she didn't have soap, and nor could she get them to rub their wounds. All she could do was rinse and dilute the acetone as much as possible.

Chrissie had arrived, along with her partner Jake, to assist. Addy explained the situation and after she'd rinsed the wounds Jake and Chrissie began applying dressings, so Robert and Wendy could be transferred to hospital.

'How are you doing, Wendy?' Addalyn asked, feeling the woman was in a state of shock and disbelief.

'I'm okay, I think. Is my face all right?'

Addalyn took in her visage. No, it wasn't all right. But it would be. One day.

'You'll get the best doctors and sort it out in no time.'

'But I'm getting married in two months.'

Addy's heart sank. 'You are? Congratulations.'

'Thanks. Me and Brian are soul mates. Knew each other at school, but then went our separate ways. He got married, so did I, and then we both got divorced for differing reasons. We met each other again a year ago and it was like life said to me, *Here you go. Have some happiness after all.*' Wendy tried to smile. 'Do you have a mirror? I want to see.'

'I don't. But there's no point in looking at it right now.'

'Is it bad?'

How to answer?

'It looks very sore.'

'Brian loves my face. Tells me every day I'm beautiful. Will he still do that, do you think?'

Addy hoped so. She hoped that, whoever this Brian was, he was the type of kind, loving man who would see past the burns and the scars that might remain and still want to marry the Wendy he'd fallen in love with.

'I'm sure he will.'

'This is our second chance at happiness. If he doesn't… Well…' Wendy blinked slowly, her eyes starting to glaze over.

Addalyn looked up in time to realise that Wendy was about to pass out. She called to Chrissie for help and they caught Wendy and lowered her to the ground, placing her in the recovery position and applying an oxygen mask to her face. She might have just fainted. It might just be shock. But they would monitor her blood sugar, her BP and her airway, just in case.

Addy was pushing the fluids, squeezing the bag, when something exploded. Instinctively, protectively, she covered Wendy's body with her own.

The boom was deafening, and smoke and a horrific stench filled the air. Blinking, cowering slightly, she turned to check on her colleagues. They were fine, but shocked. All of them were as they turned to look behind them. Part of the factory had gone up in smoke and the fire crews were trying to beat back the fire.

Ryan.

But she had no time to worry about him. No time to run and make sure he was safe. She had her priorities. Robert and Wendy... Chrissie and Jake.

Wendy was slowly coming round, having missed the explosion completely. She groaned as she came to. 'I feel sick...'

'You passed out. But you're okay. Stay lying there. We're going to transfer you to a trolley and get you off to hospital.'

'Can you call Brian?'

'Of course. Once you're safely in the ambulance.'

'Is he okay?'

'I'm sure he is. Where does he work?'

'In the admin office.'

Addy was soon transferring Wendy onto a trolley, getting her strapped in for the switch to the ambulance.

'Whereabouts?' It was best to keep her patient chatting. It was also a good way to keep an eye on any neural issues.

'The admin office here.'

Addy stopped briefly. 'Here? Where you work?'

'Yes.'

Addy turned to look at the building. Half of it was a blackened wreck, with smoke and flame billowing from all window cavities. Was that the admin office? Or part of the factory? No point in worrying Wendy until she had to.

'Give me his number and I'll pass it on to the paramedics. They can give it to the hospital, and they'll try to contact him for you, okay?'

'Okay.' Wendy smiled, her gaze content and dreamy.

Clearly the strong painkillers were working well.

Painkillers and anaesthesia were a blessing. They took the pain away. The hurt. The grief. For a while you were blissfully unaware. Reality would always come crashing back in at some point, but in that moment they would feel fine.

Addy had no idea if Wendy's future had been eliminated or not. She hoped it hadn't been. She hoped that Brian had escaped the fire and that he would meet Wendy at the hospital and hold her hand through all her painful debridement and surgeries. That he would stand by her side at their wedding and tell her she was beautiful, as he always had.

But she couldn't know for sure.

In her peripheral vision, she saw someone waving madly. She turned to see Paolo, flanked by two other fire crew, carrying an unconscious fireman away from the smoke and flame.

Her stomach flipped and churned.

And she ran towards the casualty.

CHAPTER TEN

THE FIREMAN STILL wore his oxygen mask, so she couldn't see who it was. She raced towards them, watched as they got clear of the danger and laid the man down on the pavement.

Addy fell to her knees at his side and wrenched off the mask, her heart thumping crazily.

Please don't let it be Ryan. Please don't let it be Ryan!

It wasn't Ryan.

Relief hit her like a tsunami—and then immense guilt. It shouldn't matter who it was. One of Blue Watch was hurt. Hank Couzens. She didn't know him all that well, but she did know he had a wife. Three kids. Two boys and a newborn baby girl. Any of Blue Watch or any first responder getting hurt was horrible.

But still, relief was her overriding feeling as she placed the oxygen mask back over Hank's face and began a primary survey.

'What happened?'

'He was caught in the blast. Got knocked backwards into a wall. He banged his head pretty bad.'

She examined his head and his neck. She

couldn't feel any depressions, nor any movements that might indicate a fractured skull, and Hank wasn't conscious to tell her if anything hurt. But she had to assume there were injuries she wasn't aware of, and so she wrapped a cervical collar around his neck to immobilise his head and spine in case of hidden injury.

Addy checked his arms and legs. Nothing seemed broken. His abdomen was soft, as it should be. Hopefully, he was just concussed. She radioed for one of the ambulance crews to make its way to her position and when it came helped get him onto a spinal board and into the vehicle that soon roared away, sirens blaring.

She let her gaze fall upon the burning building. The fire crews were still aiming their water hoses at it and she wondered which one of them was Ryan. How many more times would she have to stand there and wonder if he was okay? This wasn't meant to be happening to her any more. He was only meant to be a friend. And yet already she cared for him deeply.

Maybe I need to put up bigger walls?
Maybe I need to cut off contact altogether?

It had been a fierce blaze and Ryan was sweating thoroughly by the time he emerged from the site, his job done. All the flames were out and the site had been doused with enough water that no spark would survive, no matter what.

Wearily, he pulled off his helmet and lifted his face to the waning sun, grateful for the small measure of cool breeze upon his face. He stood there for a moment before moving forward towards Paolo, towards the rest of his waiting crew.

He saw Addalyn there, too, nervously biting on her fingers.

He couldn't imagine how difficult this shout must have been for her. It had been no picnic for those inside, tackling the blaze, but knowing now what she had gone through with her brother and Ricky, he knew watching any fire get out of control must be difficult for her.

'You okay?' Paolo asked as he got closer.

'Yeah. All done and dusted. I think the source of the fire was in the east wing of the building, but Investigative Services will figure that out for sure.'

With any big fire like this, the fire service investigated the cause and origins of the fire. It was useful in criminal or arson prosecutions to have their evidence and skill.

'Okay. There's water over there—get it down you and then we'll head back.'

'Cheers, boss.' He gave Paolo a small salute and grabbed a bottle of water, necking half of it before he drew level with Addy. 'Hey.'

She didn't look happy. She looked nervous. On edge.

'You're all right?'

'Yeah. Just tired. Smelly. Looking forward to

a good shower.' He tried to laugh. To make light of the situation.

She nodded. 'I bet.'

'I hope you weren't too worried about me.'

'About you? I was worried about all of you! I had to send Hank off to the hospital.'

'Hank? Damn. Is he okay?'

'He was unconscious. Caught in the blast.'

'I didn't know.' He felt bad then. Before, all he'd wanted was a shower. Now all he wanted was to go and visit his friend. Make sure he was okay.

'I thought it was you. When they brought him out he had his mask on. For one minute…' she breathed in, then out, steadying her voice '… I thought it was you.'

He stared at her, realising in that moment that she cared for him as deeply as he cared for her and how scary that must be for her. He felt guilty. As if he was somehow torturing her because of his choice of job. But what could he do? He'd never been the kind of guy to want to work in an office. He liked jobs that required the use of adrenaline. The army. The fire service. He couldn't imagine any other life. That wasn't who he was.

'It wasn't. I'm fine.'

She nodded again, not actually looking at him, and he could see in that moment that she was fighting tears. That she was fighting a huge torrent of emotion.

'I like you, Ryan. I do. And I adore your daughter. But… I can't do this again. I can't stand there and watch and wait for you to be brought out on a stretcher or in a body bag. I just can't.'

'Addy—'

'No. I can't. I'm sorry. I have to protect myself here.'

And she turned and walked away from him.

He watched her go, shocked. They were hardly in a relationship with one another—they were just friends. Very good friends. Maybe this job had been too much? Any of his call-outs had the potential to be fatal and some people couldn't handle that.

But what about *her*? What about *her* job? She was a HART paramedic—she put herself in danger, too! She might lose her life one day, doing the job she loved, and then *he* would be the one left without *her*!

Did she ever think about that?

Because he thought about it all the time. And being left alone again did not appeal at all!

CHAPTER ELEVEN

LIFE WAS SO much better without Ryan.

At least that was what Addy kept telling herself every time she felt her thoughts wandering to him. Perhaps if she told herself enough times then it would be true. It would be like when someone kept telling you that you were ugly. After enough times, you'd begin to believe it. This had to work in a similar fashion.

I don't need Ryan and life is so much better without him.

So why was she sitting at her sewing machine, missing him like crazy, and working on Carys's tiger costume? The head-piece was like a hood, but she was trying to put ears in, and eyes, and create some teeth, so it looked perfect, and it just wasn't working.

It's because I need to fit it on Carys. See exactly where the eyes and ears need to go.

But she couldn't go to their house. Couldn't visit. Because she needed this space from him. It was better this way. Before either of them got in too deep. Addy had sensed where their relationship was going. Yes, they were fine as work colleagues, and great friends, but her own feelings had been heading in a totally different direction when it came to Ryan and his daughter. They were like the little family she'd always dreamed of having. The almost perfect guy and the perfect little girl. Of course she'd begun to fall in love with them. Put water in front of a thirsty person and eventually they'd drink it even if they were told the water could hurt them.

So she'd had to separate herself from the water. Tell herself she didn't need it.

If only I could get these ears right!

She wondered briefly if Ryan took his daughter to the park often. Maybe if she saw them she could pull the little girl to one side so that she could get her to try on the outfit, mark where the ears and eyes ought to be, and then scurry off back home?

Did I just even think that? Stalking a little girl in a public park and pulling her away to some bushes? I'm losing it here.

Addy got up from her sewing machine and began to pace the room. Maybe she should give up making the costume entirely? After all, she didn't owe it to anyone.

Except I made Carys a promise.

And that meant something.

Just because she couldn't be with Ryan, that

did not mean she could let down that wonderful little girl!

I'll just march around there, knock on the door and ask for a fitting.

Ryan was standing in the kitchen, busy making pancakes, pouring his mix into the frying pan, allowing it to spread, and then getting Carys to count to three before he would try and flip them. So far, one had fallen to the floor, the second one had caught on the edge of the pan and ripped, and now he was on the third.

'Are we ready? One…two…'

The doorbell rang.

'Three!'

He flipped the pancake and it landed perfectly. Typical. But he didn't want to leave it on the heat, where it would burn, so he shifted the pan off to one side and pointed at his daughter.

'Don't touch it, okay? I'll be back in a minute.'

He wiped his hands on a tea towel and threw it over his shoulder as he headed towards the front door. He had no idea who was calling, but he was waiting for a parcel delivery. Maybe it was that and he needed to sign for it? He'd ordered Carys a scooter—a special treat. He needed to feel good about himself, and maybe get out of the house more. Stop moping about Addalyn walking away from their friendship.

Okay, so maybe it had become more than a

friendship. Even though, technically, they hadn't done anything romantic. But the thoughts and the feelings had been there. The wishes. The yearnings. The whole shebang.

He'd felt strangely upset after that factory fire, when she'd told him she couldn't be his friend any more. He'd understood why, but spending time with Addy had begun to bring him out of his shell again. He'd not been able to remember the last time he'd felt so happy. As if he were part of something special.

And damn straight they'd had something special—even if they hadn't kissed. Not on the lips, anyway. He'd kissed her cheek, and each and every time he'd wondered what she might do if he turned and kissed her on the mouth. But he'd not done it. Afraid to ruin what they had. That fledgling relationship. Both of them still cautious…both of them teetering on the edge of taking flight, not wanting to fall.

But fall he had. He'd fallen big time.

Buying his daughter a scooter was something he hoped would take his mind off the fact that he wouldn't get to see Addy again except at work.

He yanked open the door.

And his mouth dropped open.

Addalyn.

She stood there looking beautiful, despite the furrow in her brows, and despite the hardened, determined look in her eyes. She held a bag at her side and looked not at him but somewhere just over his left shoulder.

'I need to borrow Carys.'

Borrow Carys? Right. Of course. That seemed perfectly natural.

'Addalyn... Borrow her for what?'

'For a fitting. For her tiger costume.'

'Oh... Oh! You're still making that?'

'Of course! I'm not going to let her down when I promised.'

'She's just inside.'

He stepped back and watched in confused admiration as she stalked past him, then paused, awaiting instruction.

'She's in the kitchen,' he added helpfully, not sure how to proceed with what was clearly a tetchy woman completely on the edge.

'Thank you.'

'You're welcome.'

He followed her through to the kitchen, pausing a few steps behind her as she paused in the kitchen doorway.

'Hey, you.'

He watched as her entire demeanour changed when she saw his daughter. A wide smile crept across her face, and when Carys looked up and saw who it was she barrelled into Addy with an enthusiasm that made him smile from ear to ear.

Just as Addy did.

Addy scooped her up and hefted her onto a hip.

'You are getting bigger every day! It's a good thing I came round to check!'

'Are you here to play with me?'

'I'm here to measure you up for your tiger costume. I've made a start on it, but I need to keep checking it on you, just so I don't go wrong.'

'Okay! Can I see it?'

'Of course you can!'

Addy and Carys headed off towards the lounge and Ryan followed, not sure how to act or how to proceed.

'Can I…er…make you a drink?' he asked, feeling that hot beverages were safe ground to tread.

She looked up at him, her face losing its smile. 'I'm not stopping that long, so no. Thank you.'

He gave a nod and realised that he was not needed there, and that Addy would probably be much more comfortable if he disappeared and left them to it.

It was hard to leave them be. Especially since he'd been missing her. It had only been a couple of days, but already he'd begun to feel it. And Carys had been asking repeatedly when they could go back to Addy's house to continue with the jigsaw.

He hadn't wanted to lie to his daughter, so he'd simply said that he didn't know as he hadn't had a chance to ask Addy about it. Which was kind of true! He'd just not mentioned the other part.

The pancake lay cooling in the pan and he turned the cooker off and began to tidy up. Clearly

Addy was more important to his daughter than her lunch. He didn't want to interrupt them, but it was agony not being able to be with her. Just in the next room!

How quickly Addalyn has become important to me.

But this was what happened to him, wasn't it? He'd not been able to keep Angharad, either. She'd walked away. For different reasons, maybe, but if their love for one another had been stronger, would she have been able to walk away so easily? Maybe he'd not given her enough space? Maybe he'd not loved her as fiercely as he ought to have done? Maybe he'd put Carys first too much and she'd felt neglected?

But wasn't that what you were supposed to do as a father? Put your child first?

The feeling of failure as a man had hit him hard when his wife had left. He'd always thought of himself as a relatively good catch. A decent guy. Hard-working. Dedicated. Loyal. But maybe he'd given too much to his job and his daughter? Had Angharad felt neglected? She'd not been too thrilled about him being a fireman, either, though in the beginning of their relationship she'd viewed it as sort of a cool thing. Maybe when the reality of life with a fireman had hit, replacing the image of a hunky, half-naked man cuddling puppies for a charity calendar, she hadn't been able to handle it?

Like Addy.

But Addy had known the reality from the start. She'd never seen him or viewed him as anything else. He'd always been a risk to her, and maybe that was why she'd never got too close?

He pottered about in the kitchen for some time. Cleaning. Tidying away. Sitting at the table with his head in his hands until he got fed up.

In the next room he could hear laughter. Carys's perfect giggling. Addy's too.

He wanted to know what was going on. He felt left out.

This is my home. Why am I hiding away in the kitchen?

So he decided to make his presence felt.

Addy was so glad she'd come to do a fitting on Carys, because clearly she'd sewed one of the main seams on the outfit wrong and it was much too big, drowning Carys in reams and folds of tiger fleece so that the little girl could barely be seen beneath it.

'Grr! Roar!'

Carys tried to sound like a tiger from within the folds of fabric as Addy tried to locate the neckline, and when she did, and Carys's head popped out through the top, they both giggled with fits of laughter.

And then the door opened.

Addy swallowed and sucked in a breath when she saw Ryan standing there.

'How's everything going? It all sounds fun.'

She gave a polite smile, trying to control her breathing and her heart rate around him. It hadn't got any easier. In fact, since she'd walked away from him and told him she couldn't do this with him any more, it had seemed harder!

'I just need to take a few more measurements.'

'Great.' Ryan settled down onto the couch and picked up a magazine that happened to be lying there.

She glanced at it. It was a kids' magazine. Brightly coloured. It looked odd to see him reading it—because surely that wasn't his reading material of choice? Was he trying to act casual and normal around her?

Addy smiled at Carys encouragingly as she positioned her this way, then that, marking out her seams with carefully placed pins. 'That's it. Don't move for a minute.'

'When can I come round to yours to do more of the jigsaw?'

'Erm... I'm not sure.'

'What about this weekend?'

'Er...'

Ryan put down the comic. 'You're off to your grandparents' house this weekend, remember? They're taking you to visit Lara and Jacob, your cousins.'

'Oh.' Carys sounded as if that was the last thing she wanted to do.

Addy smiled at her. 'Sleeping at your grandparents' house will be fun! Think of how much they can spoil you! I remember going to my grandparents' house as a child and I loved it. Nan used to make this egg custard tart that was better than you'd get in any shop. And I remember she had this horse and carriage ornament that sat in their bay window... It was actually a music box, and I would sit and play with it, and open up its secret compartment, and every time my nan would have put something inside—like fifty pence, or a sweetie, or something else for me to find.'

Carys smiled.

'And they had this cute little white poodle called Toby. He was a bit smelly, but I used to love him anyway. Do your grandparents have any pets for you to play with?'

'They have a cat.'

'What's his name?'

'Munchkin.'

Now it was Addy's turn to smile. 'What colour is he?'

'Kind of black and brown.'

'He's a tortoiseshell,' Ryan added, drawing her eye. 'He's very rare, apparently. Most torties are female, so it probably means that...' He stopped talking, looking kind of afraid to say more.

'Means that what?' she asked.

Ryan looked away from her briefly, before closing the magazine and putting it back down on the table. 'It means that he's probably sterile.'

Addy stared at him.

'What's sterile?' asked Carys.

Now she looked at his little girl. At her curious face. 'It means he won't be able to give a female cat any babies.'

Carys thought for a moment. 'Aww! That's sad. Poor Munchkin. He'd have very pretty babies. Hey, Dad, can we have a kitten?'

And the subject was changed as fast as that.

Ryan was clearly blindsided. 'Er...not just yet, sweetie. A kitten takes a lot of looking after, and it wouldn't be fair to get a cat whilst I'm at work most days and you're at school. It would be all alone.'

He was right. Addy had often thought about getting a pet, to help her deal with being alone in the house, but it just wouldn't be fair. Unless she got a rescue cat? One that was older and already housebroken? A cat looking for somewhere to spend its golden years?

'You know, Carys, I've been thinking about getting a cat,' she told her. 'I couldn't have a kitten, for the same reasons as you and your dad, but I've thought about getting an older one. Maybe bringing it home when I've got a week off or something. I do have some holiday due. That way I could use the week to help it settle in, and after that it would be fine on its own. Maybe... I don't know.'

'Could I come and visit if you do?'

Addy glanced at Ryan. His face was impassive.

'Sure. I'll let you know if I ever do it.'

She helped Carys off with her outfit, making sure she didn't get pricked with any errant pins.

'Right. Well, I'd better be off. I should be able to make some headway with this now.'

'I'll walk you out,' Ryan said.

'Oh. Thanks,' she muttered, gathering her things and heading to the front door.

She stopped there and turned to face him. Looked past him to make sure he was alone.

'I'm sorry if I was a bit abrupt earlier. I didn't mean to be. I just felt awkward. But I hope—I really, really hope—that we can get along with each other if we meet at work or anything.'

She felt awkward. Felt as if she was rambling. But she knew she'd been harsh before, and that it was only because of how Ryan made her feel.

She was hoping that, with distance, it would get easier. But standing here, right now, in this moment, staring into his beautiful chocolate eyes and looking at his soft mouth and the slight hint of stubble, made her feel that maybe she was making a mistake. He looked so good in his dark jeans and white tee. Those arms… That chest… And his hair! So perfect… I've-Just-Got-Out-of-Bed messy hair, that made her want to run her hands through it, and touch him, and stroke him, and pull him close and smell him, and...

But Ryan represented everything that was dangerous to her emotional wellbeing. Ryan was a firefighter, and he had a child. He needed someone stable to be in his life. Someone who could give him future children. She was none of these things, and yet...

'We'll always be friends,' he said now. 'No matter what.'

He had a lovely voice. Soft. Gentle. Understanding.

I want to kiss him. I want to kiss him so much!

'I really do.'

'What?' Ryan frowned.

She felt her cheeks colour. Flush with heat. 'I mean thank you. Sorry. I was...er...thinking of two conversations at once. You know how your mind drifts sometimes?' She laughed nervously.

'Mine does it all the time,' he said sincerely, staring straight back at her.

'I ought to go. Say goodbye to Carys for me.'

'I will.'

He held open the door and let her step through.

'She's welcome to come and finish her jigsaw any time.'

'And...am I allowed to come with her? Stay?'

How would she be able to concentrate on anything with him there? But how could she say no, without being rude?

'It's okay if not. I could drop her off for an hour or two and then you could call me when you want her to be picked up.'

She was grateful that he'd given her a way out. 'Or I could just walk her back,' she told him. 'Seeing as we live so close to one another?'

'Sure! She's away this weekend, though, as I said, so maybe the weekend after that?'

'Great. Sounds great. I'd love that. I could do another fitting for her then as well.'

'Or take her with you to get a cat if you choose to. She'd love that. Though it might be dangerous for me, allowing her near all those animals that desperately need homes.'

He laughed good-naturedly.

'Yeah…anyway, I'd better go.'

She pointed at the pathway, as if it wasn't clear which direction she'd be taking as she moved away from him. It was wholly unnecessary, but her brain didn't seem to be functioning very well around him.

'Of course. I'll see you around.'

'Absolutely. Yes. At work.' She nodded.

'At work. Work only.'

'Mmm…'

She stared at him a moment longer, clinging to her last vestiges of hope that if she were just brave enough all it would take would be two steps towards him to plant a kiss on his lips. After all, what harm would that kiss, in that moment, do?

Terrify him? Embarrass him? Send me down a path that I would regret afterwards?

That last one was the reason that made her pause and reconsider. Because she didn't want any more regrets in her life. She had enough to deal with. She'd lost her boyfriend because she couldn't give him children. Lost her father and brother in a tragic accident. Did she really want to lose Ryan too?

By resisting—by not kissing him, not letting this attraction thing she had going on proceed any further—she could stop any more regrets right now. They could remain friends. And that was enough, right?

'Goodbye, Ryan.'

She gave a slight smile and, using all her strength, she walked away.

CHAPTER TWELVE

WATER RUSHED FROM the hose towards the flames as Ryan held it steady, grimacing inside his helmet as his gaze took in the blackened walls, the blooms of soot, the curtains that seemed to dance as the fire consumed them from the floor upwards, the way some of the ornaments that had been in the window had either exploded from the heat or melted.

The source of the fire was the sofa. Someone had not noticed their cigarette falling from the ashtray that was perched on the arm, and it had fallen into the innards of the upholstery and started a fire.

Smoke had been the first sign. Luckily the owners had been in the kitchen when they'd noticed it, and had been able to get everybody out of the house before smoke inhalation had become a problem. But they would still need to be checked over by an ambulance crew, just in case.

There was no one to rescue here, which was great.

Their job was to extinguish the flames and stop

the fire spreading to the houses on either side, as this one was mid-terrace.

Paolo had made sure those homes had been evacuated, too, just to be safe.

Smoke billowed all around and another window shattered, allowing in more oxygen to fan any remaining embers.

The heat was incredible, but Ryan kept the hose aimed at the source until the flames began to die down and the living room became sodden.

Black licks of soot patterned the ceiling in a kaleidoscope of marks, and one part of the roof had begun to burn through. He kept an eye on it, aware of the possibility of collapse, but he had no reason to move further into the room from where he was. They had control now. They had it beaten.

Ryan grabbed the hose lock and turned off the water, bracing himself for the drop in pressure that would affect his balance. When only drips dropped from the hose-end he and his crewmate Jonno, who'd been behind him holding the hose too, began to make their way out of the devastated and ruined building.

'Fire origin was definitely the sofa in the lounge, boss,' he told Paolo.

Paolo nodded. 'At least everyone got out. That's the main thing. You can replace bricks and mortar; you can't replace people.'

Ryan nodded. Paolo was right. You couldn't replace people, even if you tried. Because everyone was different. When Angharad had first left him he'd never imagined wanting to replace her. He'd been too hurt. But lately he'd often thought about what it might be like to meet someone new.

Like Addalyn.

Carys adored her, and he did too. But she would never replace Angharad. He would always remember his wife. Always try to remember the good times they'd shared. Because life was too short to keep on remembering the pain.

Addy, in turn, could never replace her father or her brother. Or that guy she'd hoped to have babies with. In fact, she didn't seem interested in replacing anyone. Almost as if she was too scared to—which he understood. She was still in the scared phase. It would pass. One day. He hoped he would still be around when it happened. Because he believed that if she ever got brave enough, then his life with her could be something amazing!

But her fear, her hesitation, her need to flee… that worried him. Because if he was going to be with someone else—someone who would be part of his daughter's life—then he needed someone who was strong. Not someone who was a flight risk. He couldn't let Carys hope that Addy would be in their lives for good if Addy was going to run each time things got difficult or terrifying.

'Get the hoses back and pack up,' Paolo ordered.

'Will do.'

Ryan glanced over at the two ambulances that had turned up to treat the family in case of injury, hoping to see Addy. But she wasn't there. She only got sent to the really serious jobs. And even though this had been a potentially hazardous rescue, the information that had come in before the shout had told Control that there was no danger to human life. Everyone was out. A HART paramedic had not been needed on this occasion.

Maybe she was on a shout somewhere else? Maybe she was on a day off? Maybe she'd finally taken that holiday she'd said she would?

I miss her.

That was the pervading feeling. He'd got used to seeing her at work. He'd finish a job and look up to see her there. It always made him feel good, knowing that she was by his side. Knowing that she was safe. Taking care of her patients. But also knowing that she had one eye for him as well. For all of Blue Watch.

Her family.

The Tutbury cat rescue centre was practically overflowing with cats. Kittens, pregnant females, feral cats that had been captured and were being trained to get used to humans and, of course, the older, senior cats, which were kept in a different, quieter building. A retirement home of a kind.

That was where Addy had asked to go. She'd spent some time being interviewed at the front desk—about her home, her lifestyle and what sort of cat she was looking for. She'd told them about her job and her hours, and fully expected the manager to say *I'm sorry, but you're just not suitable.* But then Addy had explained that she'd got a couple of weeks' holiday booked soon, and she wasn't actually going to go away, but wanted to use that time to help a senior cat settle in. After that she'd be out for eight or nine hours each day. Sometimes more, if a job ran over, because accidents and emergencies didn't run to a neat schedule.

'But I grew up with cats,' she'd told the manager. 'My family always had them. Mostly moggies, but I do remember we once had a Russian Blue.'

'I think one of our senior cats will be perfect for you,' Letty, the manager, had said.

So she'd been escorted to the senior cats' housing unit and allowed to look around on her own. The majority of them were curled up fast asleep, as classical music played softly in the background. Each unit had a single cat in it, or sometimes two, if there was a brother and a sister, or a bonded pair that couldn't be split up. Cats of all colours. Of all types. One had an eye missing. The card attached to its cage said that Poppy had been injured in a fight with another cat and an infection had caused her to lose the eye.

There were so many sad stories. One cat had feline FIV. Another only had three legs after a traffic accident. One had been diagnosed as having cerebellar hypoplasia—a neurological condition that made it wobbly and have issues with its balance. This one was a black cat.

'Black cats are often not chosen for rehoming. People can be terribly superstitious,' Letty had said, as if apologising for the quantity of black cats she was about to see.

And there were a lot of black cats.

Addalyn was not superstitious, and as she perused the cards she also looked at the dates, wanting to know which cat had been there the longest.

And then she found him. In the last unit. Sitting in his soft bed, washing his face. Curly.

Curly had been born with anophthalmia, his card said. Which meant he'd been born with no eyes. And he'd been at the home the longest.

Seven years.

Addy couldn't imagine a cat being stuck inside this place for seven years. Seven years of classical music. Seven years of listening to people come and go, never being chosen.

He was a pure black cat, thirteen years old, and he'd come to the rescue centre after his previous owner had died.

It was a long time to be here.

A long time to go without someone to love.

A long time to go without affection.

Even though she felt sure the caretakers here

would have done their absolute best for him, she felt an affinity for Curly. She'd lost the person she loved too. She'd been left alone with no home until her father and brother had taken her in, and then she'd lost them too. And she had spent a few years without affection. Blind to love.

'We're made for each other, you and I,' she whispered, putting her fingers through the bars and making noises to try and entice Curly to the front of the cage.

Clearly he'd heard her. His other senses must be heightened because of his blindness. He came forward to sniff at her fingers, and then rubbed himself along her hand and the side of the cage, his tail in the air.

Addy smiled.

She'd found her cat.

'I'm going to take you home with me, Curly. Would you like that?'

Curly purred in response.

She spent some time with him in a special room along with Letty, who was thrilled that Curly had been chosen by her.

'He's such a special cat. We've all become so fond of him. In a way it'll be sad to see him go, but he's going for all the right reasons.'

'My time off doesn't start for another week,' said Addy. 'Can I collect him then?'

'Of course! And you're welcome to visit him as often as you'd like in the meantime.'

'Really? That's great. I'll try to pop in every day after work—if I have the time and you're still open.'

'Perfect. Shall we do the paperwork?'

'Let's do it.'

It was a mere formality. Addalyn had to promise to send the rescue centre pictures of Curly in his new home, and agree that if for any reason she couldn't keep Curly she would return him.

'I don't think that's ever going to happen, let me tell you now,' she said.

Letty smiled. 'I'm sure it won't, but it does happen on occasion, so we ask everyone.'

'Okay. I feel like he's mine already. It's going to be hard to walk away right now,' she said, stroking his soft fur. 'But I need to get the house ready for him. Get bowls and toys and a litter tray...'

'Exactly. You want to be ready when you invite someone new into your life.'

Addy looked up at Letty. She meant the cat, clearly, but she was right in other ways too. If you went into a new relationship without being ready then it was likely to fail at the first hurdle. Life was difficult enough without plunging headfirst into emotional turmoil.

She thought of Ryan and Carys. She missed them so much—which was crazy! Staying away was hard when you knew the person you'd like to spend time with was just around the corner. Literally two streets away.

When the paperwork was done, she gave Curly one last hug and then turned to leave the building. She pulled open the door and walked smack-bang into a man's chest.

'Oh! I'm so sorry! I…'

She looked up and saw Ryan. Of all the places… She'd never expected to find him *here*.

'Ryan! What are you doing here?'

He looked embarrassed, and shocked to find her there.

'Same thing as you, I'm guessing.'

'You're adopting a cat?'

'After you spoke about it Carys and I talked a lot, and we decided that it was something we both really wanted to do. Give a cat another chance at life. Give it something better than what it has right now.'

'You do have love to give,' she said with a smile, knowing the feelings he was talking about.

He stared her right in the eyes. 'Yeah… We do.'

She stared back. Taking in the beautiful darkness of his soft, chocolatey eyes. The intensity of his gaze.

'Have you chosen one, or…?'

He broke eye contact—reluctantly, she thought.

'Yeah! Curly. He's back there. Last cage on the left.' She pointed behind her.

'Mind if I take a look?'

'Sure!'

She walked with him over to the pen, smiling

at Curly as he settled himself back in his cat bed, plumping the soft pillow with his paws, purring away.

'He's cute.'

'He was born without eyes, so I think people might have overlooked him because of it.'

'Bless him… He looks sweet. He'll make you a very good pet. What other guys have we got in here?'

Addy decided to walk around with him as he considered the senior cats, even though she'd been on her way out. It seemed right to do so—and besides, Letty was still there, so it wasn't as is anything was going to happen.

'Who's this guy?'

'Girl,' Addy said, looking at the card. 'It's a female. Molly.'

Molly was a striped tabby cat. Twelve years of age.

'She has six toes on one front paw, it says here!'

'I can't see…'

Molly was curled up in her bed, slowly blinking at them. Probably wondering why there were suddenly so many people in the centre, looking at her.

'Perhaps she only shows them to people who are special?' Addy said with a smile, then laughed as Molly stood and stretched, front legs low, back end high in the air, showing off her six-toed foot after all.

'Hey, there…' Ryan put his finger though the

bars so that Molly could sniff him. 'What do you think, Addy? Will Carys like her?'

'She'll love her! She looks like a little tiger.'

'With huge feet.'

'With huge feet!' she echoed, laughing, letting Molly sniff her fingers too.

'Molly gets on very well with Curly, actually. We think they love one another,' said Letty, coming to stand behind them. 'When we let them out into the outdoor runs for some fresh air, they snuggle up all the time.'

Addy looked up at Ryan. 'That's sweet, isn't it?'

'It is.' He turned to Letty. 'Could I get Molly out to see how she reacts to me?'

'Sure.'

And so they sat on the floor and let Molly explore them. The cat sniffed here and there, intrigued by the other pens, but eventually she came over to Ryan and Addalyn, walking between them, tail held high, as they stroked her and she began to purr.

'She's perfect,' said Ryan.

'You're made for each other,' agreed Addy, feeling a mixture of emotions. She was happy for Ryan and Carys that they would have a cat so perfect for their home, but also strangely jealous of Molly. Because she would get to spend so much time with her favourite people. People she herself was trying to train herself to stay away from.

Ryan arranged with Letty that he would call

again when he knew his shift pattern and would have a decent break to help settle his new pet. He filled in the paperwork, and Addy listened as Letty asked him the same questions and had him agree to bring Molly back if she got too much for any reason.

As they left the centre, Ryan walked next to her through the car park towards her car.

'Well, this is me,' she said, pulling her car keys from her bag. 'Where's yours?'

'I walked.'

'You *walked*?'

He laughed. 'This is going to sound silly, but the house is so quiet without Carys there. It feels strange being there on my own.'

'I understand that feeling.'

'I thought it would take up more time if I walked.'

'Less time home alone?' she asked, smiling.

'Yeah!'

She knew, intimately, how that felt. It had been her life for years, and she could see he was struggling with it.

'Do you fancy going for ice cream?'

The question was out of her mouth before she could think about the dangers. And after she had asked it she told herself it would be fine. They would be in public. Nothing would happen. They were just friends. That was all.

'Oh!' he said. 'You don't have to...'

'No. I mean it. We're okay, aren't we? We can have an ice cream. A walk in the park. It doesn't have to mean anything. Besides, we're going to be like in-laws.'

'In-laws?'

'Because of our cats. They're in love. Or whatever,' she said, with a hint of embarrassment.

She could not quite believe what she had just said. She looked at him and shrugged, as if to say *You know what I mean.*

'That's as good a reason as any,' he said.

Addalyn drove them to the high street and parked near the fancy ice cream parlour that had opened up there. She'd been meaning to try it for ages. It was called One Scoop or Two? and as usual it had a queue out through the door, despite the time of the year.

Addy had heard nothing but good things about the place. Apparently it was owned by an Italian whose grandfather had begun a gelato shop in Naples. It had become two shops, then three, then four. She'd heard people say the flavours and the texture of the ice cream was out of this world!

She'd not had an ice cream for years. She'd used to go out for ice-cream all the time with Nathan. He'd loved nothing better than a raspberry ripple every weekend. More often than not she wouldn't have one herself, preferring a sorbet or nothing at all, but right now she wanted to have an ice cream with Ryan and go for a walk in the park. Spend time with him now that she'd run into him. It was as if this moment was an unexpected gift and she didn't want it to end. Not yet.

As they got closer, they spotted a board listing the flavours—all the usual suspects, but also butterscotch, cake batter, green tea, maple, watermelon and bubblegum. Lots of unexpected things.

'Do we try something new or stick with a favourite?' Ryan asked, turning to smile at her.

His smile made her feel special.

'Go for whatever you fancy,' she told him.

His look, with a raised eyebrow, made her blush slightly.

When they got to the front of the queue, Ryan ordered one scoop of matcha tea ice cream, with a second scoop of maple. Addy ordered cake batter and butterscotch.

They were delicious! Smooth, and not too overpowering in flavour. Sweet, without being sickly.

'Want to try mine?' Ryan offered his cone to her.

She looked directly into his eyes as she leaned in, took hold of the cone and licked it. The matcha was amazing! Slightly bitter, but sweetened enough that it wasn't off-putting. She offered her own cone and he tried her flavours, looking directly at her as he licked the ice cream.

There was something almost sexual about it. Almost hypnotic. Addy couldn't tear her eyes away from his gaze. And then he mentioned he liked the cake batter more than the butterscotch and she remembered they were sharing ice cream in a public space.

'It's good, isn't it?' she said.

'It can be scary, trying something new, but sometimes you can find something that you don't ever want to let go of,' he said.

She nodded. He was right. In, oh, so many ways.

With food.

Experiences.

People.

Ryan was like a drug at this point. She wanted to be with him so much. To experience him. To taste him. Smell him. Envelop herself with him. But he was dangerous. He represented a threat to her mental and emotional wellbeing. He could hurt her. Not intentionally. But it might happen anyway.

Could you experience someone like that in moderation and not go mad?

People in the park were enjoying the last of the warm days. There were families, couples, people jogging or walking their dogs. Here in the park, surrounded by greenery, unable to see the town, it felt as if they were in a small bubble of peace and serenity. It was nice. Soothing. And she understood completely why people liked being surrounded by nature.

Here she could forget. For a moment, at least. Pretend that all was right with the world and that being here with Ryan was fine. Meant to be. A gift that she should cherish, because soon it would be over. Soon he would go home and she'd be alone again. Without him. But right now, at this moment, it was perfect—because he was here by her side.

'I love it here,' she said, as their steps carried them past the lake.

'It's very peaceful.'

'Makes a change from our jobs, doesn't it? We're so frenetic there. Running on adrenaline, with a million thoughts and possibilities and prospective dangers rushing through our heads...lives on the line...other people relying on our life-or-death decisions...'

'We can be like everyone else here. Normal.'

'Yeah...'

A dog raced past them and leapt into the lake, sending a group of ducks quacking in all directions as the owner bemoaned the fact that her dog was now wet and would stink up the car.

They both smiled as the dog came trotting out of the lake, pleased as punch, its tongue hanging out of its mouth.

'When does Carys get back?' she asked.

'Sunday evening.'

'Not long to go, then?'

He glanced at his watch. 'Too long. I always think it'll be good to have a break from being Dad. Nice for Carys to spend some dedicated time with her grandparents, being spoilt, but I always miss her when she's gone.'

'Do her other grandparents ever see her? Angharad's parents?'

Ryan shook his head. 'They did once. Had her for the day. But…it didn't work out. They said it was too stressful—that they were too old to look after a little one. Which didn't make any sense as they were only sixty-something, and in very good health. Maybe it was too stressful for Angharad? Having the daughter she gave up on spending time with her parents?'

'I'm sorry. Carys has lost more than a mother… she's lost grandparents too.'

'You can't change other people's decisions. If they've decided they can't have you in their lives, then that's how it's got to be.'

She pondered on his words. She had made a decision not to have Ryan in her life because of her deep growing feelings for him. Yet here she was. Walking through the park with him. Sharing ice creams and not yet ready to walk away.

Because every time I walk away I think it won't hurt this way. But it does. It does.

'Do you ever wonder if she thinks she made a mistake?'

'Angharad? No. If she did, I would have heard from her. Texts. Calls. Maybe even emails. But I get nothing—so, no, I don't think she has ever doubted herself.'

Addy doubted herself. She yearned to protect herself, but she also yearned to be with Ryan.

What am I doing?

'Hey, look, the boat place is still open! Fancy sharing a rowing boat with me? I'll row,' Ryan offered.

She'd finished her ice cream, so…

'Sure!'

She still wasn't ready to walk away. Today was a gift.

The rowing boats were all lined up alongside the small lake, and after they'd paid the boat guy took them over to one that had faded red paint on the hull, and held it steady as they both clambered in.

Ryan began rowing and took them out onto the water, dark green and cloudy. She tried not to notice the muscles flexing in his forearms as he rowed.

'Wow. This is so peaceful,' she said. 'I don't think I've been out on a rowing boat before.'

'You haven't?'

'No. I've been on a cruise ship, though.'

'Exactly the same.' He smiled. 'This is your captain speaking. We have just left port and we'll be making our way around the local lake today. Conditions are sunny and warm. Wind is blowing at a slow two knots and the onboard entertainment for today is…er…me.'

Addy laughed at him and he laughed back.

'You're silly.'

'I am. One hundred percent.'

'I like you, Ryan Baker.'

He paused as if to consider her. 'I like you, too. A lot.'

Her heart beat a little faster at his words and she felt her cheeks grow hot, so she looked away, at the people walking in the park, not knowing what to say next.

The fact that he liked her too…it meant something. It meant that what she was feeling wasn't stupid. She wasn't imagining this attraction between them. They both felt it. It was a war they were fighting, both not sure which tactic to use next to ensure they both survived and came out of it relatively unharmed.

Because being hurt was scary.

Being hurt was difficult and hard.

Painful.

The recovery process could be long and arduous, and she'd been injured so much already. She wasn't sure how many more injuries her heart could take. Which was why she tried to eke out small moments in which she could be happy.

Like today.

Like now.

With Ryan.

There was a small island in the centre of the lake, thickly populated with trees and bushes, and Ryan headed towards it. 'There's a folly on it somewhere. Want to go and find it?'

'Why not?'

He rowed their boat towards the island, looking for a small bay or inlet they could use, and on the far side of the lake they found one. A small nook, barely noticeable behind a weeping willow that overhung the shoreline. As they approached Ryan slowed, so that they could move aside the curtain of overhanging branches. It was like being transported into a new world. A hidden world. With the willow muffling the sounds from the lake. After he'd moored up, Ryan pulled the boat higher onto the shore and then proffered Addalyn a hand so she could disembark.

She took his hand delicately, her skin electrified by his touch and guidance as she stepped onto dry land.

It was quiet here. Darkened beneath the canopy of trees.

'Are we allowed to be here?'

'Probably not.'

'How do you know there's a folly?'

'I read about it once. When we moved here. This lake, and the land around it, used to belong to a duke or something.'

'I didn't know that. I've lived here all these years and never knew.'

He smiled at her and reached for her hand as they walked along the narrow path through greenery that was waist height.

'He built the folly for his wife. In remembrance of her.'

'Sounds like he loved her very much.'

'She died young, I think, and he pined for her for the rest of his life.'

Addy felt his pain.

'Can you imagine that?' he asked, stopping to turn to her.

'Which part?'

'Being so overwhelmed by grief that you couldn't enjoy life any more?'

She stared into his eyes. 'Perhaps he didn't know how to?'

'Perhaps he never met the right person who could help him.'

Addy didn't know what to say. She didn't have a folly for her father and Ricky, but there was kind of a shrine in the fire station. She didn't want to be like this duke! Pining for those she had lost for her entire life. Because what kind of life would that be? She still had to find happiness. She still had to find the thing or the person that would give her joy. And right now the people who did that for her were Carys and Ryan.

And what would her dad say if he could see her acting this way?

Take the chance, love! You can't live a life alone.

'Ryan, I...' Her voice faltered.

She wanted to tell him, to let him know that she hadn't walked away before because it was his fault in any way. But for some reason the words wouldn't come. They caught in her throat. She wanted to say how much he meant to her, how he made her feel, and just how she wished she could be what he needed her to be.

'It's okay. I know,' he said, smiling at her. 'You make me feel that way too.'

She sucked in a breath. What he was saying… what he was admitting… This was more than friendship. This was scary territory. But territory that she just might be brave enough to enter all the same. With him.

The folly emerged up ahead. A stone building once white, but now cobwebbed and grey, with moss, lichen and ivy creeping over its old bones. Parts of it had crumbled away, proving time was not a kind mistress to memories either.

Was Addy going to make a lifetime of grieving?

Or create something new?

Something to celebrate?

Ryan led her up the two stone steps and turned to face her. She held her breath. Afraid and terrified of what he might say or do. And yet at the same time eager and keen for something to happen. Because this was a magical place. She could feel it in her bones. In her blood. In her heart.

'Addalyn…'

'Yes?'

'You mean the world to me… I want you to know that.'

'You're important to me, too.'

'I think we could have something amazing together if we let it happen.'

She nodded, unable to speak now. He was saying all the right things. The things she'd dreamed of him saying. But it was scary stuff. Heady stuff.

'Will you let it happen?' he asked. 'I won't do it unless you want me to.'

Consent. He wanted her consent. He knew she'd be scared and, despite how much he wanted her, he needed to make sure that she was happy. Was determined that she should be the one to decide if this proceeded or not.

She'd tried walking away and it had hurt.

What would happen if she allowed him to take his pleasure with her?

Surely the world wouldn't be cruel enough to take away a *third* firefighter from her life?

She gazed deeply into his dark eyes. Stared intently at his lips. Imagined them on her own.

They were hidden from the rest of the world here. In this spot that symbolised a lost love. Maybe they could find love here? Change the significance of this place even if it was just for them?

'Kiss me, Ryan. Kiss me.'

A slight smile curved the edges of his lips as his head lowered to her hers and the rest of the world drifted away.

CHAPTER THIRTEEN

HE'D NOT INTENDED to bring her to this island. He'd not intended to run into her at all! Discovering her at the Tutbury cat rescue centre had simply been lucky. Right place. Right time. And now they were both looking forward to rehoming Molly and Curly.

Getting to spend time with Addalyn was an unexpected bonus. First ice creams, then a rowing boat, and now this.

He knew she was scared, and he'd refused to kiss her without her consent. Because there was no way in hell he was going to do anything that would send her scurrying for safety again. He didn't want to represent danger to her. He didn't want her to view him as some sort of risk. He needed her to see him as who he was. Ryan Baker. A man who could offer her happiness and joy if she let him.

The kiss deepened.

He felt her sink against him, heard almost a purr or a growl of pleasure in her throat, and it was enough to stir his senses and make him giddy.

His hands sank into the hair at the nape of her neck as hers came to rest at his waist. He couldn't remember the last time he'd kissed a woman in this way. There'd been no one since Angharad, and their relationship had been dying a slow death since the birth of Carys. She'd not wanted him near her. He'd felt confused. Rejected. All he'd wanted to do was love her. Protect her. Revel in the tiny person that they had made together. But she'd pushed him away, and for a long time he'd felt unworthy. Unworthy of another's love. Unworthy of another's attraction.

Until Addalyn Snow had come into his life.

She loved his daughter almost as much as he did, and he had to be careful not to let that sway his feelings for her. But it was hard not to. She was sexy, brave, clever, beautiful, funny, loving… His desire for her was a powerful thing, and having been told once to stay away when he had feelings for her had been one of the most difficult things he'd had to deal with. And it had come just as he'd been beginning to accept that Angharad's behaviour and desertion from their marriage was more about Angharad than it had ever been about him.

It wasn't my fault.

That had been a huge thing for him to accept. To realise that he did have something to offer a woman, but it was about finding the right woman.

And Addalyn, he felt, could be the one.

He needed to let her know just how much she meant to him. This wasn't just a snog…this wasn't a mere attraction. This was more. Ryan wasn't playing games. He was serious. All his life was serious. Personally and professionally. And Addalyn got that, because hers was too.

Maybe she was the only one who could ever understood him?

When he came up for air, he gazed into her eyes, noted her full, soft lips and knew he wanted more.

'Are you all right?'

She shook her head. 'No.'

That startled him slightly. Had he misread the signals? She'd wanted this, hadn't she?

'I don't understand…'

She smiled. 'I want more. I want all of you. Here. Now. In this place.'

'I don't have protection.'

She turned her head, kissed his hand. 'I can't get pregnant, and I haven't been with anyone since Nathan.'

'I've not been with anyone since Angharad… Are you sure about this?'

'I'm the most sure I've ever been about anything. *You* make me sure.'

He stared deeply into her eyes. Into her soul. She wanted this as much as he did.

'All right then.'

He kissed her again, but this time he released the chains and did not hold back the way he had a moment before.

His fingertips found the buttons of her blouse and began to undo them.

One by one.

Until his fingertips found flesh and heat.

And after that…?

He wasn't sure he could think straight.

Being with Ryan was everything and more. Her senses were firing as if they were being electro-cuted. Short-circuited. Her entire system was in a frenzy of pleasure and ecstasy. He was gentle, yet strong. With the right amount of rough and the perfect amount of dirty.

She'd never made love outside before. She would never have imagined that being out in the open, during the day, in the middle of a public park, with no soft beds or soft lighting, would be anything but uncomfortable. But in actuality she felt no discomfort at all. Because being with Ryan felt so right that it would never feel wrong.

Afterwards, she lay in his arms, feeling so re-laxed, so sated, so happy… She found herself won-dering what she'd been worrying about. Nothing this amazing could be bad. Her thoughts from before, her entire rationale for staying away from Ryan, were faulty.

They had to be.

She curled into him, her head upon his chest. 'I don't think I ever want to move from this space.'

She felt his smile. Heard it in his voice.

'Nor me. But we only get an hour on the boat, so…'

Addy laughed. 'They can bill us. I'll split the charge with you.'

'Let's stay out here all day, then.'

He gave her a small squeeze and pressed his lips to the top of her head. A little gesture, but it meant so much. Their relationship had taken a step forward and now they were on uncharted ground. But that little kiss told her that whatever waters they waded into next he would be by her side. That they would do it together.

'I wish we could…'

A small gentle breeze blew over her skin and she shivered.

'Cold?'

'It's getting cooler.'

They agreed to go and both stood up, straightening their clothes and making themselves presentable again. Ryan held her hand as they made their way back to the boat, and he helped her into it before pushing it back into the water and hopping in himself.

The boat rocked slightly, then settled as he rowed them out from beneath the weeping willow and back into the sunshine. The goosebumps on her arms dissipated beneath the last warming rays of the sun as he took them back to the boat house, apologising for being late. The guy was fine with it, and they soon got back onto dry land and headed towards the car park.

At her car, they got in together and looked at one another.

'Want me to drop you off at your place?' she asked.

Ryan smiled. 'You could. Or…'

'Or?' she asked with a smile.

'Or you could come back to mine and stay the night. Carys is away, so she won't know, and I rather like the idea of getting you into a hot shower. What do you say?'

Ryan. Naked and wet. In a shower.

'Sounds perfect.'

'Then let's go.'

Addalyn came padding downstairs in her bare feet, her hair wrapped in a towel, wearing his bathrobe. Never before had he ever considered his bathrobe sexy, but with a naked Addalyn in it… It sure the hell was!

He put down the knife that he was using to chop peppers and turned to greet her, pulling her into his arms and kissing her deeply. He simply could not get enough of her.

They'd made love all day. In the shower. In his bedroom. Once against the wall and a second time in the actual bed, where he'd taken his time to take her in and marvel at how she responded to his touch, how she tasted, how she felt… He'd almost forgotten about his own pleasure. He'd just wanted to see her enjoy hers—until she'd rolled him onto his back and trailed her lips down his body, and then he hadn't been able to think at all.

'Can we stay in this bubble?' she asked.

'At least until tomorrow we can. Carys comes back in the evening.'

'You want me to be gone by then?'

'Of course not! But I don't want to give Carys the wrong idea about us.'

'That's fair. I don't want to confuse her either. Best wait until there's something to tell her.'

'Do I tell her that I've seen you?'

'I don't mind that.' She smiled.

'Okay. I'll tell her we chose cats together. That's a cute story.'

'I'd miss out the island chapter, though,' she said.

'And the shower one? And the bedroom one?'

She laughed. 'Of course! Mmm…something smells good. What are you making?'

'A sauce to go with pasta.'

'You don't just use something out of a jar?'

'Carys isn't the biggest fan of tomatoes, so I usually make my own.'

'Can I help?'

They spent a merry hour in the kitchen. They nearly got derailed when he spoon-fed her a taste of his pasta sauce and his thoughts ran away with him slightly, but their hungry bellies kept them back on track and eventually they sat down to eat in front of the television and watched a movie. An adventure flick about art thieves and a heist.

When had he last sat down and watched a movie with a beautiful woman in his arms? Ryan wondered. When had he last felt this content? He couldn't remember. Even with Angharad there had always been an *edge*. A slight nervousness. A feeling of never being fully relaxed.

But with Addalyn he felt as if he could be himself. Totally. Wholeheartedly.

Why was that?

Actually, he didn't need to question why. He knew. His feelings for Addalyn ran deep. He cared for her. Adored her. Maybe he even loved her?

But he wouldn't say so. Not yet. Because he didn't want to scare her away—not when they'd just spent practically all day and evening in each other's arms. A declaration of love now might be too much!

He smiled to himself and laid his head against hers. 'Happy?'

'Very much so.'

Her answer was all he needed.

CHAPTER FOURTEEN

ADDALYN WAS PACKING up the car, going through her checklist to ensure the vehicle was ready for her shift, when a call came over the radio—a fire at a four-storey building. Multiple casualties, residents trapped inside.

Her blood ran cold, as it always did, as she listened to Control reel off information. There was a possibility that the incident had begun after some kids had been found mucking about with fireworks in one of the flats. She recalled going to that building once before, as a fledgling paramedic. It was always overcrowded, meaning many lives could possibly be at risk.

'Roger, Control. ETA six minutes.'

She turned to look at the town and saw grey-black smoke beginning to billow up into the sky over on the western side. It was rush hour, too. So the roads would be busy. Already she'd calculated the fastest route in her head, and thought about any shortcuts she could take to maybe get there quicker to liaise with the fire crews and the police.

And to think she'd come to work this morning floating on cloud nine...

Her weekend with Ryan, though short, had been the most wonderful couple of days and the most amazing, mind-blowing night. When she'd left him she'd practically skipped away from his house, and for the first time ever had returned to her own home without that feeling of dread, that sense of isolation, she usually felt.

She'd gone home, taken a shower, sewn a bit more of Carys's costume and then spent the rest of Sunday evening retiling the backsplash in her kitchen. She'd changed so much in the house now and made it her own. The repairs and decorations had really helped with the sense of comfort she felt there now. It was as if she'd given the place a new lease of life. The way Ryan was making her feel like a new person. And Addy liked who he had helped her become.

But now they were back to reality—and their reality was that their jobs were to assist with the accidents and emergencies of life. Life or death situations.

Addalyn raced through the traffic, her lights flashing and her siren blaring as she weaved through parked cars and the vehicles that had come to a standstill to let her pass. She forged her way down the centre of one road as cars pulled over to each side, and had to perform an emergency stop when an old lady stepped off the kerb, thinking the traffic had stopped to let her cross.

Maybe the lady couldn't hear or see very well,

but she almost jumped out of her skin to see Addy sitting there, waiting in her car, lights circling red and blue.

And then she was going again—always aware, always on the lookout for dangers as she drove. It would be no good if she got into an accident herself when she was needed somewhere else. She glanced at the dashboard clock. Two minutes down. At least another four, maybe three, if the traffic lightened somewhat.

'Scene update. Fire services now on site. Police are cordoning off Bart Road.'

'Thanks, Control.'

Ryan was working today—she knew that. Day shift. He was probably already there, along with Paolo and the others.

She tried not to think about him having to go inside a building that was aflame. It was his job. He knew what he was doing. They all did. They were trained for these situations. They practised. People like Ryan and the rest of Blue Watch, they kept calm and steady. They knew what they had to do and how. Knew that fires were tackled in certain ways.

'The best-known method is something we call direct attack,' she remembered her brother saying. *'We aim to suffocate the flames at the base of the fire. To do this effectively we must have a clear line of sight to the fire. Then there's the combination attack method, where we use direct and*

indirect attacks on the fire to help fight the over-head gases and the flames as well. Or we have the two-line-in method, when we have to deal with a fire in high winds. A solid stream and a fog nozzle work best with those.'

She could see her brother now, sitting at the breakfast table, trying to show her using the salt and pepper shakers as props and the cereal boxes on the table to represent a building.

That very day he and her father had been killed. She remembered because afterwards, when she'd raged and screamed and cried, someone had patted her on the back, trying to soothe her with words.

'They knew what they were doing. It was just an accident.'

There were high winds today, so maybe the two-line-in method, then?

Traffic began to back up and clog as she got closer and closer to the site. She had to honk her horn a couple of times, to get people to move, and slowly but surely she crept her way up the road.

Bart Road sat at an intersection with Williams Street, and now she could see what she was responding to. One of the blocks of flats—a four-storey building called Nelson House—was billowing thick, black, choking smoke from almost every window. The outer walls were darkened with soot and orange flames roared furiously out of the ground-floor and second-floor flats, moving upwards.

'Holy hell...' she muttered, looking for a place to pull over and park.

Her gaze was caught by a couple of firemen helping two people away from the building. Probably residents, they were coughing and choking furiously, their skin smoke-stained, and one of them, she could see from her position, had burns to the back of one hand.

Addy leapt into action, slinging on her high-vis vest and getting the attention of two other paramedics to attend to the burn victims.

The fire crews behind her had many hoses pointed at the building, jets of water streaming in through the broken windows to the flames within. Around the site sat many people, shocked, stunned, coughing—residents who had escaped.

But how many were still left inside? Trapped? Terrified?

'Sit rep?' she asked Paolo as she reached his side.

They spoke a shorthand that might seem strange to others, but it was something they knew well, and he brought her up to speed.

There were still people trapped inside and he'd sent in some men to rescue them.

Addy looked at the building, at the fire that still seemed to be out of control and raging inside, and tried to imagine having to walk into that. How had her dad done it? Her brother? How did Ryan do that?

'Who have you sent in?'

'Ryan and George. White Watch have sent in two, as well.'

Ryan was inside.

She tried not to focus on that one piece of information. It would not do her any good to imagine him inside that hell on earth.

'How many do we think are still trapped?'

Paolo looked at her with a frown. 'Unknown.'

'So how will they know when to stop looking?' she asked with concern.

It was a question she had never asked before, and she'd only asked it because she knew Ryan was inside. She didn't want him in there any longer than was necessary. She wanted him *out*.

Paolo glanced at her with a raised eyebrow. In all the time they'd worked together she'd never sounded worried, because she'd always slip into work mode. Businesslike. Stoic. Calm. She'd never shown fear before, and he'd clearly heard it in her voice.

'When the fire gets too great or the building becomes unstable.'

Unstable.

Immediately she saw in her mind's eye the building that had collapsed right in front of her, killing her father and brother in an instant.

Addy felt sick.

'Right.'

Paolo turned to her. 'Addy? If this is too much, then maybe you should—'

'It's not. Too much. I'm fine. I have a job to do.'

And she walked away from him towards the gathering patients to assess and triage quickly, so that the other paramedics knew who to attend first, who were walking wounded and who were fine.

It was odd that even with something like this there were people who could walk away without a scratch. It had happened when Ricky and her father had died. People had lost their lives that day. Firefighters and residents alike. But some had escaped without even a cough.

She tried to concentrate. Tried to do her job. But with every shout, every yell, every call, she looked up, distracted, often needing to pull her focus back to her patients with grim determination and fight the desire to stand in front of the flames and yell Ryan's name.

Addy dealt with burns and smoke inhalation. A broken wrist from a fall. A fractured femur in someone who had leapt out of their second-storey window. And then she heard it. A rumble, a crash. And she turned to see a new cloud of thick, black smoke puff up into the air as the roof of the building collapsed and flames leapt into the air.

'Ryan!'

The heat was unbearable. Ryan was sweating non-stop, and he could barely see anything through the thick smoke as he emerged from the stairwell to check for anyone stranded on the top floor. People had told him there were others still up there. Residents trapped in their rooms. They'd heard the screams.

The stairwell was the safest place in the building. Made of concrete, it couldn't burn—not like the rest of the place, which had seemed to go up like dry tinder. It was an old building. Built during the sixties. No doubt with cheap materials and the work contracted out to save money. And this was the result. A highly flammable building, overflowing with families and children. Pets.

He'd already guided out three families. Saved over twenty lives.

'You must get Mustafa! He lives in flat forty-two. He's bed-bound and blind!' someone had told him.

He'd promised he would, sending the families down the stairwell and out into the fresh air to be treated whilst he remained and surged upwards. George trailed behind him. George was a seasoned firefighter and they worked well together. He trusted his life to him.

The fire was working its way up through the ceiling of each flat now, and when he emerged onto the fourth-floor corridor the smoke was thick and black and flames licked from beneath the doors of one or two flats. Yes, they would check flat forty-two—but they had to check *all* the flats, just in case.

He kicked down a door and called out to see if anyone could hear him over the noise of the consuming flames.

'Is there anyone in here?'

He looked in the narrow kitchen, the living space, the bedrooms, the tiny bathroom, edging along the sides, avoiding the gaping holes in the burnt-through floor. He knew lots of people would hide in bathtubs, after soaking themselves with water. But this flat was empty.

Eventually they got to number forty-two. Smoke poured out from beneath the door and Ryan burst it open, calling out.

And he heard a voice.

It was weak. Croaky. Scared. Coming from the bedroom.

'Stay where you are! We're coming for you!' he yelled, unsure if the old man would hear him.

Fire had burst through a hole in the floor in the main hall and the smoke was thick and dark, billowing like steam from a kettle.

George followed behind him.

'Let's maintain our exit!' Ryan shouted.

George nodded as he checked through a doorway to find a small storage area, cluttered with towels and cleaning equipment.

He watched as George grabbed the towels and took them into the bathroom to douse them with water. If they reached Mustafa in time, they might help in getting him out.

There was the sound of something breaking. They paused their advance long enough to check it was nothing in their immediate vicinity and then continued on down the hall to the bedroom at the end.

The hall was cluttered. Filled with newspapers and scientific journals. It would all go up like tinder if the flames reached them, effectively blocking their exit. They had no time to lose.

Ryan surged forward and checked the bedroom door, to make sure it wasn't hot before he opened it, and when he did he saw an old man, huddled in bed, coughing and afraid.

'Mustafa?'

'That's me.'

'I'm Ryan, and I've got my friend George with me. We're with the fire service and we're going to get you out of here, okay?'

'That would be wonderful, my friend.' He coughed again. 'COPD.'

'Or maybe just smoke.'

Ryan smiled as he wrapped Mustafa in the wet towels, apologising for how they might feel.

'I would rather be wet and cold than dry and burnt.'

'Good attitude. Right. Let's get out of here. Can you walk?'

'No.'

'Then we'll carry you—but we must be quick. We're losing flooring with every second.'

'Do what you must.'

Ryan hefted Mustafa into his arms. He barely weighed anything—all skin and bone. The wet towelling seemed to weigh more. He checked their exit, saw that it was still viable, and began to thunder his way back down the corridor. There was another crash behind him and he turned to check on George. He was right behind them, but the flames that had begun licking up through the floor had reached the pile of papers and magazines and was beginning to feed.

And that was when he saw it. Down at the bottom of the pile, leaning up against the wall, almost hidden by the journals, was the top of a gas canister. A canister of oxygen.

Mustafa's COPD.

'Damn. Let's go!'

He practically ran from the hall, out of flat forty two and into the stairwell, and then began running down the stairs as quickly as he could.

When the whole building was rocked by an explosion Ryan fell to his knees, rolling expertly to protect Mustafa from the concrete steps, and all around him the world went black. A high-pitched ringing noise was the only thing he could hear after he briefly banged his head against the floor and came to a stop.

And then all vision was lost as thick plumes of dust and dirt and soot filled the air.

CHAPTER FIFTEEN

THE TOP FLOOR collapsed in on itself, it seemed, and Addy couldn't stop herself from screaming out Ryan's name.

'Ryan! *Ryan!*'

She surged forward, only to be held back by Paolo.

'No, Addy. You can't go in there!'

'But Ryan's in there. It can't happen again! It can't!'

Paolo wrenched her back and stood in front of her, staring into her eyes until she made eye contact with him.

'Stay. Out. Here. Let us deal with this.'

Addy began to shake, shudder and cry. She couldn't think. She couldn't deal with this. It was just so awful, so horrible...

Ryan could be in there—could be trapped. Maybe pinned down by a concrete pillar or a beam? Maybe knocked unconscious somewhere, unaware of the flames getting closer? Or maybe he was dead already? Killed by smoke inhalation so severe that he had been completely asphyxiated.

She sank to her knees, realising that she was

of no help now. She couldn't help anyone. That wasn't what she was there for. All she could do was stare at the building and feel such pain that…

She blinked. Were those figures coming out of the flames? Or were her eyes just so watery from her tears that she was imagining things?

It looked like two figures. One was misshapen and blackened…the other looked like a fireman…

And then the smoke cleared as they got closer and she realised it was two firemen, but one was carrying a man wrapped in towelling. He lowered the man to the ground, once they were clear, and pulled off his helmet.

Ryan!

Addy surged forward and ran to him, almost knocking him over when she reached him.

'You're safe!'

He was bleeding. Blood had trickled down his scalp and dried on his face, which was riddled with sweat and soot.

'This is Mustafa. Registered blind and with a history of COPD.'

Ryan staggered to his feet to give her room to treat him and she literally had to force her brain to go into medical mode. She didn't want to treat anyone. She wanted to make sure that Ryan was okay. He looked so pale…he looked as if he was going to pass out.

'Ryan, are you okay?'

'I'm fine. I'm just…' And then he sank down

to his knees and keeled over, his eyes rolling into the back of his head.

She wanted to go to him, but couldn't. Other paramedics rushed forward to treat Ryan as she dealt with Mustafa, getting him further away from the burning hazard that was his home and towards the ambulances.

She knew she couldn't give him full-flow oxygen as that might be damaging to someone with COPD and could cause hypoventilation. But Addy almost couldn't concentrate. Couldn't do her job. Her mind was focused on Ryan and whether he was okay. He had a head injury—that was clear.

She managed to get the attention of another paramedic and passed the care of Mustafa on to him. He deserved the best medical attention he could get and she was distracted. Couldn't think. Was panicking.

And that made her useless.

She could not do her job because of how she felt.

Addalyn sat in one of the horrible plastic chairs that hospitals always provided in their waiting areas. It was green, with a questionable bleaching stain on the seat, but that didn't matter. She sank into it gratefully, her mind awhirl, as she tried to gather her thoughts and think straight for the first time since the fire.

She had a decision to make. Maintain her relationship with Ryan or walk away. And, as much as she loved him—for she knew now that she did—she knew that being his girlfriend, or whatever she'd be classed as, meant facing days like today. Over and over again.

Did she have the strength?

Or she could walk away. End it now. Create distance between them. Go back to being just colleagues and try to forget the last couple of days of bliss. Consider them a gift. A cherished memory. Walk away to keep her sanity and what remained of her heart intact.

But first she needed to know that he was all right. His head injury meant that he'd been taken to Accident and Emergency. He'd probably be needing stitches or glue for his scalp laceration, and maybe an X-ray to check for any skull fractures—though he hadn't shown any signs of anything as horrific as that.

He'd been lucky.

They'd been lucky.

But was it lucky to have gone through what she had?

Because to her it had felt like hell. That building's top two floors had slowly collapsed, as if in slow motion, and the horror of losing her dad and her brother had come rushing back. The feeling it had engendered in her—hopelessness…impotence…pain—was not something she wished to experience ever again.

A doctor holding a patient's file came into the waiting area. 'Addalyn Snow?'

She stood, felt her mouth dry. 'Yes?'

'I'm Dr Barclay. Come with me, please. Ryan is asking for you.'

That meant he was okay, right? Conscious. Capable of forming sensible sentences.

She followed Dr Barclay to a cubicle where a dirtied, smoke-stained Ryan sat on a bed, having a gauze patch taped to his head by a nurse.

'Eight stitches and no broken bones,' she explained as Addy looked at her in fear. 'He's got a tough skull, this one.'

'Numbskull, more like.' Ryan grimaced, giving a half-smile.

His eyes had lit up at seeing her approach, but she could see in his face that he didn't know what she was going to say.

'I'm sorry if I scared you.'

Sorry. He was sorry. But it wasn't his fault. He'd been doing his job, after all, and he'd saved that old man. Risked his own life for it. He didn't have to apologise.

She did.

'I've never been so scared in my life.'

She stared at him, wanting to say more, but the nurse was still there, and the doctor, so she turned to them.

'Would you mind if I have a moment alone with him, please?'

'He's all yours,' Dr Barclay said. 'He can go home. You're a hero,' he said to Ryan, turning and shaking his hand before he and the nurse left.

Alone in the cubicle with him, Addy felt terrified all over again. 'I'm glad you're all right.'

He smiled. 'So am I.'

He held out his hand to her, as if he wanted her to be nearer. To hold her. Touch her.

And she wanted that too… But she couldn't do it.

Addalyn took a step back—a hint at what was to come.

'I'm very glad that you're all right. More than you could ever know. But—'

'Addalyn, you don't have to do this.'

'Don't I? I had to stand there and watch again— *again, Ryan!*—as a building collapsed into itself with someone I love inside.' She laughed bitterly, feeling tears burn her eyes. 'Losing one person in a fire is a tragedy, two is ridiculous—but three? Do you know what it does to a person to stand there and feel helpless? To watch as their world crumbles before them, knowing that they can't do a thing about it?'

'It must have been awful.'

'It was. Words aren't enough to explain how I felt in that moment when I thought you might be dead. How much I hated Paolo for holding me back from running into a burning building. And how relieved I felt when I saw you emerge from the flames.'

'But I'm okay, Addy. I'm okay!'

'I know. And I'm glad. But I can't keep doing that to myself, Ryan. I can't keep putting myself through that. We work in the same field; we know the risks. I couldn't do my job!'

'What?'

'My job. I needed to help Mustafa and I *couldn't*—because you'd collapsed and my fear for you stopped me from doing the one thing in this life that I can do well! I love you. I do. But being in love with you is painful, Ryan. It hurts. It burns me. And I can't be burned any more.'

Ryan looked down at his shoes. 'I'm sorry.'

'Don't be. You did your job. As the doctor said, you're a hero. And I'm so glad that you get to go home to Carys tonight.'

'I'd love to come home to you too.'

She smiled sadly as tears dripped down her face. 'Me too. Goodbye, Ryan.'

And she turned and walked away, her heart breaking as she walked away from the man she loved.

The man who caused her too much pain to be with.

CHAPTER SIXTEEN

LIFE WASN'T THE same after Addy walked away. At first he'd felt shock, then anger. He couldn't help what he was! He was a firefighter and she'd known that from the get-go. He was not going to change the job he loved. And with the anger had come the thought that maybe he and Carys were better off. His daughter had already experienced a flaky mother—she did not need to experience her dad's new girlfriend not being dependable either.

Because that was what he knew he needed. Someone he could rely on. Someone who would love him no matter what. Who would accept what he did for a living and not ask him to change. He'd never ask Addy to stop being a paramedic. Stop doing her job! He would be better off finding someone who was strong enough to be by his side for all of life's little foibles. Not someone who was going to run every time life got hard.

But even though he kept telling himself that he didn't need Addalyn in his life, and even managed—sometimes—to convince himself of this, every time he saw her at work it was hard. He tried to not be around when she was on the scene, avoided her as much as he could, but today was one occasion when he'd just got his timings wrong.

'Addalyn.'

He gave her a nod of acknowledgement, hardening his heart, telling himself that being polite was more than she deserved.

But ye gods, it was hard. Seeing her was a torture. He might have told himself he no longer needed her, but he wished somehow he could make his body and his heart understand that. He wanted to stand by her. Touch her. Let their fingers intertwine and share a smile with her. Just to see a smile on her face when she looked at him would be enough...

'Ryan! I didn't know you were on today.'

They'd been called to a small village where, after a particularly heavy amount of rain, there'd been a flood from the local river. It had broken its banks and flooded streets and homes and many people had had to be evacuated.

'I think most of us are here,' he managed to say, knowing that fire services from many local areas had sent in teams of rescuers.

'Of course. And...you're well?'

'Very.'

'No problems since the head injury?'

'No.'

'That's good.' She nodded, all businesslike. 'I'm

very pleased to hear it. Don't let me stop you. I'm sure there's plenty you need to be doing.'

'We've finished evacuations. I think we're going to try pumping some of the water out of the infant school.'

She nodded and turned away from him. Dismissing him? She was discussing her plans with Paolo, as she often did when she arrived on scene.

He hated it that she'd made him feel as if he was surplus to her requirements. That he was nothing.

'That's it?'

Addy turned to look at him, alarm showing on her face. She glanced at Paolo, before looking back at him. 'I'm sorry?'

'That's all you have to say to me?'

'I'm not sure there's anything else to say, Ryan. We've said everything.'

Paolo took a step between them. 'Baker. You're needed at the school.'

He gave Ryan a look that said *You don't want to do this.* And, no, he didn't. But he couldn't help himself.

'Did you ever think about *me*?'

She looked shocked.

'Did you ever think about how much *I* worry about *you*? *Your* job? You're a HART paramedic! You could be hurt! You could die! And I'd be the one left behind. Me and Carys. And I can't let my daughter be abandoned again.'

Ryan stalked away, feeling a fire in his blood

that took some time to douse. He occupied himself in pumping out the water from the school and focused hard on the job. By the time he'd done everything he could, Addalyn was gone.

He knew he should have handled it better, but things had still felt so tense between them.

When he got home he tried to be present for Carys, who was happily chatting about a project she was doing at school with her best friend Tiffany. Something about a poster… But it was hard to concentrate.

'Dad?'

'Huh?'

'I asked you a question and you didn't answer me.'

'Sorry, honey. I was miles away. What was the question?'

'When can we go back to Addy's house? I haven't finished my jigsaw,' she said.

'Um…that might be difficult for a little while. I think she's busy.'

'Oh. Can we knock on her door and ask?'

'Er…maybe. Not tonight, though.'

'Of course not! I'm in my jammies, silly.'

She began to giggle and carried on playing with a doll that appeared to be having a tea party with some teddy bears.

'But we can go and see her new cat when she gets it, can't we?'

He nodded. 'I'll have to ask. She'll want it to

have time to settle in, I should think, and get used to its new home before strangers can come in and cuddle it. It might be scared.'

'Like Molly might be when we get her?'

'That's right. She'll need time.'

He thought about what he'd said. Did Addy need time because *she* was scared? And, if so, time for what? To process? To understand? To change her mind? Had he been too hasty in judging her? She'd been through a lot.

He tried to imagine how she must have felt when he was trapped in that building. She'd lost her father and brother the same way. Watching from outside. And that day she'd known it could happen again, with him inside. No wonder she had panicked! She must have felt awful!

Guilt filled him at the way he'd raged at her earlier, and he wondered if it might be too much to give her a ring and ask for a chat? Clear the air a little? Maybe let her know that he would still be there for her if she needed him?

But he didn't get time to ring.

Because the doorbell did.

Addy stood on the doorstep and tried to calm down, her nerves doing nothing to still the trembling in her body. She'd thought long and hard about her decision back at home, sitting there and staring at Carys's completed Halloween costume. She wanted Ryan's little girl to have it. After all, a promise was a promise, and she would never, ever want to let Carys down. But also she felt she needed to talk to Ryan. Clear the air.

His lights were on, and she thought she could hear the TV, so they were definitely in.

She raised her hand and pressed the button for the bell again, hearing it ring inside.

Oh, God, what am I doing?

Through the patterned glass she saw Ryan walk towards the door. Her heart began to hammer even faster and her mouth went dry.

I won't be able to speak.

Ryan pulled the door open and stood there, looking gorgeous as he always did. He wore a black crew neck jumper and blue jeans. His feet were bare.

He stared at her in surprise. 'Addalyn. We were just talking about you.'

Oh. Okay.

'You were? Nice things, I hope?'

Her voice lilted upwards at the end of her question.

I sound Australian.

'Carys was asking about coming to see Curly and working on her jigsaw—but don't worry… I told her you were busy and that Curly would need time to settle in.'

'Oh. Right. Okay.'

He seemed calmer than earlier.

They stood there for a moment, staring at each other.

'What's that?' He pointed at the parcel under her arm, wrapped in rose-pink tissue paper and tied with a pretty bow.

'It's Carys's Halloween costume. I thought I'd bring it round. A promise is a promise, after all.'

He nodded. 'Want me to call her?'

'I would like to see her. I've missed her.'

He turned and shouted behind him. 'Carys! There's someone here for you.'

Someone.

'And I'd like the chance to talk to you also, if I may?' she added.

Now he turned back to look at her, confused, but he didn't get a moment to say anything because Carys barrelled past, straight into Addalyn's arms, and clung on like a limpet.

'Addy! I've missed you! Can I come round soon?'

Addy laughed and gave her a squeeze. 'Of course you can! You're always welcome in my house.'

'We're getting a cat called Molly!'

'I know you are.' She playfully tapped Carys on the nose and set her down on the ground. 'Listen, I need to talk to your dad. Why don't you take this?'

She passed Carys the now crumpled tissue-wrapped gift.

'For me?'

'For you,' she said with a smile, watching with

joy as Carys ripped it open to gasp in delight and awe at her tiger costume.

'It's got a tail, Dad—look! And teeth!'

'I can see! Carys, honey…why don't you head upstairs and try it on for size?'

'Okay!'

Carys dashed up the stairs, her little feet thudding so hard it sounded as if a herd of wildebeest was passing through.

Ryan stepped back and invited her in.

She passed by him and headed to the lounge, feeling apprehensive. The easy bit was done. The hard part might just be impossible…but she had to try.

'Thank you for letting me speak to you.'

'I wasn't sure you'd ever want to speak to me again.'

'Of course I would. I would always want you in my life. I've just had to deal with some pretty strong emotions. Ones that I wasn't ready for. Or didn't think I was ready for.'

He nodded and she took a seat, whilst he settled onto the couch opposite her.

From upstairs there came a thump.

'I'm okay!' they heard Carys yell, causing them both to smile.

Addy sucked in a breath. 'I panicked. Before. At the fire when I thought you were trapped, and then again afterwards when you made it out.'

'You panicked when I made it *out*?'

'Yes. Because I knew in that moment that if I stayed with you I would have to experience that feeling over and over again.'

'Right. Of course.'

He looked disappointed. But she needed to lay the groundwork before beginning her explanation. 'I've taken a long time to think about things. Work through my emotions. I even went to a couple of therapy sessions. And that stuff's not cheap.'

She tried to make a joke. Lighten the mood.

'We all could probably do with therapy,' said Ryan. 'No matter who we are. What did you learn?'

'That I felt like a nobody.'

'A nobody?'

'I don't like feeling helpless. Or out of control. I've had it all my life, Ryan. I couldn't have children, no matter what I tried, and I lost the chance of having the family I'd always dreamed of. I thought getting pregnant, having a baby, would be easy. Natural. It wasn't. And when Nathan left me for someone who could give him the family he craved, it made me feel like…'

Her emotions threatened to overwhelm her in that moment.

'A nobody?'

She nodded. 'Like I was worthless. Useless. That I had nothing to offer anyone. That's why my job has always been so important to me. Because I make a difference! I save lives!'

'So do I.'

'Yes. You do. And that's why I know I could never ask you to change who you are—because it's important. Very important. Both our jobs are.'

'I'm glad you agree.'

'When I lost my father and my brother I felt so incredibly alone. I felt so incredibly unseen. All I did was work. I told myself that I couldn't get close to anyone. That I couldn't love anyone. Because everyone I loved left me alone and hurting and in pain. It seemed simpler to be alone.'

'And then I came along...'

She smiled. 'You came along. You brought life and warmth back into my life. I was scared of it. Scared of what you'd made me feel for the first time in ages. I felt like I mattered. Like I wasn't alone. And you brought me so much joy! So when I thought I'd lost you, I felt like I was going to lose myself all over again...when I was just beginning to live.'

He reached across for her hand. Squeezed it.

'In that moment when I thought I'd lost you I felt like the world was trying to tell me that it would take everyone from me, and I stupidly thought that if I stayed with you then I would lose not only you, but Carys, too. That something horrible might befall you. And I didn't want to be responsible for that.'

'It wouldn't be your fault.'

'I know. The therapist said the same thing. She

made me realise that my life alone was more painful than my life with those I love. That I cannot control what might happen to anyone and that's okay. I'm not meant to be in control of that. But that doesn't mean I need to punish myself by staying away from people. I deserve love, and I deserve to feel like I matter. And, more than anything in the world, I really, really want to matter to you and Carys.'

'What are you saying, Addy?'

'I'm saying that... I love you. And that terrifies the hell out of me. But what terrifies me more is being alone. I feel we have something that could be amazing and beautiful if we let it. If you're willing to forgive me.'

She let out a shuddering breath. Had she said it the way she'd wanted to? No. Even though she'd practised her speech in the car, and at home, and on the walk over she'd forgotten bits. Missed bits out. Got confused. But she had spoken from her heart, and she hoped that he would appreciate that even if he sent her packing. Because she'd had to try. Had to say sorry. Even if he wouldn't allow them to be together.

'Thank you. For all you've said.'

He paused for a moment. Was he practising his own speech? she wondered.

'I was hurt when you walked away. Confused and angry. Which I want to apologise for. I should never have shouted at you like that. In front of

Paolo, too. I thought it might make me feel better to blurt it all out, and it did for about a second, but afterwards…?' He frowned. 'Every time I try to love a woman she walks away from me. So I know how you feel!'

He smiled ruefully, before his face grew serious again.

'I vowed to never bring a woman into my daughter's life unless I knew I could depend upon her—because it's not just me that's had someone walk away from them. It's Carys too. She had a mother who one day may make *her* need therapy. *Why wasn't I good enough for her to stay for?* I didn't want her to think that you'd done the same thing, so she doesn't actually know that we fell out.'

'Oh. Well, that's good. But I would never have stopped contact with Carys. I would have asked you to consider letting me stay in her life even if I couldn't be in yours.'

'Really?'

'Yes! Absolutely! I could never imagine walking away from her. Her mother doesn't know what she's missing…what a wonderful person she is.'

Ryan smiled. 'I knew in my heart that you would never abandon her, whatever happened. But I have to know you're serious, Addy. Because my job is going to continue to make you feel helpless, and I don't want to be the cause of any more emotional pain for you.'

'I am serious. Relationships aren't easy, Ryan. None of them. They're difficult and they're painful and they're upsetting at times. But people get through because they're a family. I've lost my family twice now, but being with you and Carys has shown me what it's like to be in one again, and I'd rather be there, in a family, loving one another and being terrified, than not be in one. Love is worth the risk. *You* are worth the risk. Carys is worth the risk. I want to love you both. I want to spend my days with you. My nights. I want to soak up every minute with you and enjoy it. Even the difficult parts. I won't run. I won't hide. Because I can't leave you. And even if you do one day have to leave me I will be there. For our daughter.'

He smiled. '*Our* daughter?'

'She feels like mine. I can't stop thinking about her. Worrying about her. This time away from her has been torture.'

Ryan moved from his seat opposite to the one next to her. He stroked away her tears and tucked a strand of hair behind her ear.

'You're amazingly strong—you know that?'

'I've been cowardly.'

'No.' He shook his head. 'You've been incredibly brave. All that you've been through… It would break some people.'

'It almost broke me.'

'But it didn't. You *fought*. For yourself. For us.'

'Us? Is there going to be an us? I can't give you any more children.'

He smiled again. Broadly. 'Yes. There is an us. There has *always* been an us. And there is more than one way to make a family.' He kissed her. Lightly. 'I have always loved you, Addalyn Snow. And I'm going to continue to love you until the end of our days.'

Her heart soared. 'I love you too.'

At that moment Carys jumped into the room with a roar, her tiger tail swinging behind her.

They both laughed, and Ryan swooped her up into his arms.

Addy moved to stand beside them. 'You look amazing. It fits perfectly.'

'We all fit perfectly,' said Ryan.

And he leant in and kissed Addalyn on the lips.

'You kissed! Does that mean you're my daddy's girlfriend now, Addy?'

'Only if you say it's okay,' she answered.

They both looked at Carys.

'Yay!'

And Carys pulled them both in for a hug.

EPILOGUE

THIS WAS THE perfect place. Now was the perfect time. Addy stood waiting in the bathroom on the morning of her wedding day. Waiting and staring suspiciously and hopefully at a small piece of plastic perched on the back of the loo.

She'd never dared to hope. Never dared believe that the happiness she already had could actually *increase*. Because life with Ryan and Carys, making her new family, had been *everything*.

Of course there'd been moments. Scary moments every time she'd got called to a shout that she knew Ryan was on, knowing that at each job he would be running towards danger, whereas she and anyone who wasn't a fireman would be staying away from it.

But she'd dealt with it. Grown accustomed to the fear and now called it her *'old friend'*. Because that fear only existed because *love* existed. And she was going to hold on to that love for as long as she could. She trusted in Ryan's training. In his skills. He'd survived the army. He'd survive the fire service. And if he didn't—if he got injured or, worse, killed—then she would be devastated, of course. But she would still have had their love, she would still have the many memories that they'd made, and she would still have Carys.

And maybe—just maybe—if this pregnancy test confirmed what she already suspected, she would have someone else to love and care for, too.

The doctors had never found a reason for her infertility, but she'd just accepted that she was infertile. But these last few weeks she'd become tired...occasionally had some tension headaches. And she'd felt bloated, sometimes nauseous. But she had put all that down to the stress of planning her wedding. To sampling lots of cakes—red velvet, lemon and poppyseed, fruit, sponge, chocolate... They'd tried them all.

And then her period hadn't come. It had to be stress, right?

But her period had continued not to come, and yesterday she'd gone out and secretly bought a pregnancy testing kit to use today, on the morning of her wedding.

It seemed right.

It seemed perfect.

Only what if it was negative?

Would it spoil her day?

Their day?

Today was a day for unadulterated happiness, and she didn't want anything to mar that!

But she had to know. She couldn't wait another minute.

Addy picked up the test, squeezing her eyes shut and praying to whatever gods there were that this test would be positive. That just for once life would work out for her and give her every iota of happiness it could. That things would go right. That she might go from being no one to being a beloved girlfriend and a beloved fiancée, to being a stepmother, and then to an actual *real* mother to her own child.

It didn't matter that Carys wasn't hers. That she wasn't her biological child. Addy felt that she was hers and always would. She loved Ryan's daughter as if she was her own, and grieved for the fact that she'd never known Carys as a baby. Never held her in her arms and rocked her to sleep.

Please. Please. Please!

Her wedding dress was hanging from the shower rail, having been steamed the night before. Her make-up lay waiting for her to apply it. Her hair, wrapped in a towel on her head, awaited the stylist.

And Addy waited too. Fear lingered for one last moment, pausing her hand, before she finally found the strength to open her eyes and look at the result.

Addalyn gasped, putting her hand to her mouth in shocked disbelief.

Pregnant.

Laughing, crying, she looked at her reflection in the mirror. She was going to have a baby! Ryan's baby! A sister or brother for Carys! The family she had always longed for.

Everything was perfect.

Addalyn felt happy. Serene.

Not calm. But buzzing!

How to tell Ryan?

When to tell Ryan?

After the service?

At the wedding dinner?

As they danced their first dance?

She tried to imagine his face when she told him. When they told Carys.

They would have picnics. With their children chasing one another as Ryan and Addy sat on blankets on the grass and held hands, watching them.

Happiness and joy were now hers for the taking.

Life only got better and better.

* * * * *

*If you enjoyed this story, check out these
other great reads from Louisa Heaton*

Single Mom's Alaskan Adventure
Bound By Their Pregnancy Surprise
Snowed In with the Children's Doctor
The Brooding Doc and the Single Mom

All available now!